MANCHESTER
BY
THE SEA

MANCHESTER
BY THE SEA

A SCREENPLAY BY

KENNETH LONERGAN

THE OVERLOOK PRESS
NEW YORK, NY

This edition first published in paperback in 2021 by
The Overlook Press, an imprint of ABRAMS
195 Broadway, 9th Floor
New York, NY 10007
www.overlookpress.com

Abrams books are available at special discounts when purchased
in quantity for premiums and promotions as well as fundraising or
educational use. Special editions can be created to specification.
For details, contact specialsales@abramsbooks.com
or the address above.

Cataloging-in-Publication Data is available from the Library of Congress

Book design and type formatting by Bernard Schleifer
Printed and bound in the United States

FIRST EDITION
ISBN 978-14683-1661-2
1 3 5 7 9 10 8 6 4 2

INTRODUCTION

It's always a mixed bag writing an introduction to your own work, since of course the work is really supposed to speak for itself. On the other hand, this is a screenplay and not a movie, and most of what goes into a movie does not appear in the screenplay no matter how faithful to the script the finished film may be. Reading the screenplay of a movie you like can sometimes be a flat experience, especially if you're looking for anything like the feeling you get from seeing the film. There are many exceptions, of course; the screenplay of Paddy Chayefsky's *Network,* for example, is almost as much fun to read as the movie is to watch, but for the most part screenplays are written to be shot, not read.

However, reading a screenplay does have its own rewards. Even when a favorite movie scene turns out to consist of just a few short, apparently colorless lines of dialogue, it may disappoint as a strictly aesthetic experience, but it can still serve as an interesting map on which to chart the differences between the written scenes and the executed film. Was it the performance, the lighting, the costumes, the sound effects, the editing, or the music that made the scene so effective? Maybe it was the dialogue after all. How does the tone change from script to screen—what was left out and what was added and how did it affect the final result? How completely or incompletely did what the writer saw and heard at his desk end up on the screen? How did the director enhance, supplement, discard, ignore, or rely on the script as written?

Hollywood professionals and cinephiles in general are fond of repeating the old adage that movies are a visual medium—and so they are. More than plays, more than opera and, because of their scale, more than television. But this famous platitude is often misunderstood and misstated to suggest that there is something intrinsically uncinematic about dialogue. For me, the best sense in which movies are a visual medium before anything else is the sense in which movies bring to their antecedents in the theater and photography a visual range of expression no other media can provide. (Even this distinction leaves out the tremendous impact of sound design, another unique branch of moviemaking whose antecedents have been transformed by the cinema for its own unique ends.) And while it's perfectly true that all movies are made of images, many great movies pretty much put the camera in front of the actors as simply as possible and let them talk.

At either extreme you can run into problems. As soon as I feel like I'm watching a filmed play, I lose interest immediately. An imaginatively filmed play, like *A Streetcar Named Desire,* is different. But the same thing happens to me when I watch a film that is no more than a visual bag of tricks. If the writing is no good, I don't really care what the camera is doing. It's interesting to note that even a visual medium like film can more easily survive bad or boring imagery than it can bad dialogue or a boring plot, but it's really a false dichotomy no matter how you look at it. Despite the insistence of most screenwriting manuals, or the well-known views of filmmakers like Alfred Hitchcock and Stanley Kubrick among others, the primacy of the image does not suggest any kind of prescription for how much talking people should or shouldn't be doing in the movies generally. Kubrick and Hitchcock were both in love with images, yes, but they knew very well that without a decent story and dialogue the image is hopelessly compromised. They both said so often enough.

Many of the world's great movies are loaded with dialogue: *Network, His Gal Friday, Dodsworth, The Miracle of Morgan's*

Creek, and *Casino,* to name a few at random. Others are masterpieces of verbal brevity, like *Barry Lyndon, The French Connection, Dr. Zhivago, Sounder,* and many more. No movie can weather truly bad performances either, and very few movies would very good without good ones, no matter how beautifully the shots are composed. Where would *Casablanca* be without the dialogue, performances, plot, hats, raincoats, music, production design, cinematography, and lighting? The fog alone in the last sequence does almost as much for the ending as the dialogue, but I'd rather have the dialogue than the fog if I had to choose. And spare as it is, I'd lose all the dialogue in *2001: A Space Odyssey* sooner than I'd compromise the image.

Where my own work falls on either side of this imaginary divide, I really can't say. I started as a playwright, and so far, the screenplays I've written have been heavy on the dialogue. The visual side of filmmaking, however, is inescapably fascinating, even in the early writing stages. But whether as a piece of writing that evokes the finished film, or as a kind of reverse guide to just what the actors, editing, and sound design have done to animate the writing, I hope this screenplay can provide the reader with something of value. If not, you can always just watch the movie.

MANCHESTER
BY THE SEA

EXT. MANCHESTER HARBOR—SEA. DAY.

A small commercial fishing boat heads out of Manchester, Massachusetts, toward the open sea. JOE CHANDLER, late 30s, is in the wheelhouse. In the stern are LEE CHANDLER, JOE's younger brother by five years, and JOE's son PATRICK, about 9 years old. LEE and PATRICK are kidding around in a friendly way while JOE steers.

SEVEN YEARS LATER—THE PRESENT

EXT. BOSTON—QUINCY—APARTMENT HOUSE. DAY.

It's a cold winter day on a narrow street.

In front of a small apartment building, LEE sweeps away the old snow on the pavement, then sprinkles salt in front of the building. He is 40 now, wearing janitor's coveralls under his weatherbeaten winter jacket.

INT. BATHROOM. DAY.

LEE works on a leaky toilet while MR MARTINEZ, 50s, a big man in an undershirt and glasses, stands by watching.

> MR MARTINEZ
> I don't know why the hell it keeps
> dripping. All night long, drip, drip.
> I've had the fucking thing repaired
> ten times.
>> LEE
> You need a new stopper.

MR MARTINEZ
Oh is that it?

LEE
See how it's rotted around the edges?
It doesn't make a seal, so the water
drips into the bowl. I can bring you a
new one tomorrow, or you might
want to consider replacing the whole
apparatus.

MARTINEZ
What do you recommend?

LEE starts putting away his tools and cleaning up.

LEE
Well, I could replace the stopper first,
and if that doesn't work, then I
would come back and replace the
whole apparatus.

MARTINEZ
But you don't have a professional
recommendation?

LEE
It's really up to you.

MARTINEZ
Well, tomorrow I got my sister-in-law
coming over with my nephews . . .
and I gotta take my car in . . .

LEE waits while MR MARTINEZ works out his schedule.

INT. BASEMENT. DAY.

He organizes the trash cans and recycling in the basement.

INT. APARTMENT BUILDING HALLWAY. DAY.

He vacuums the hall with an industrial vacuum cleaner on a
fifty foot yellow extension cord.

EXT. QUINCY—ANOTHER BUILDING. DAY.

A different apartment building on a similar street.

INT. MRS GROOM'S APARTMENT. DAY.

Standing on a ladder in a small grandmotherly apartment,
LEE changes a light bulb in the very small bathroom. MRS
GROOM, 70s, is on the phone outside the open bathroom door.

> MRS GROOM (*On the phone*)
> No, it's my sister Janine's oldest
> girl's bat mitzvah . . . No, I look
> forward to being bored to death . . .
> No, the girl doesn't want it, the
> father doesn't want it. I don't ask.
> Seven hours in the car, I could really
> slit my throat . . . Oh, well, the little
> girls are charming.

EXT. QUINCY—A SLIGHTLY MORE UPSCALE STREET. DUSK.

A marginally more upscale building.

INT. BATHROOM. DUSK.

LEE looks down at a stopped-up toilet. Behind him is MARIANNE,
slender, 30s, attractive, wearing everyday around-the-house
clothes.

> MARIANNE
> I am so sorry. This is so gross.

> LEE
> It's all right.

He plunges her toilet carefully and methodically.

LATER—He wipes up the floor. MARIANNE comes in.

> MARIANNE
> Oh Lee, you don't have to do that,
> honestly.

LEE

That's OK.

MARIANNE

Well—God. Thank you so much, I am
so sorry.

LATER—He is washing his hands in her bathroom sink.
He hears MARIANNE talking on the phone O.C.

MARIANNE

No, tell him to come! . . . Okay, yeah
. . . But Cindy, I have to tell you
something. I'm like, in love with my
handyman. Is that sick? . . . Have you
ever had a sexual fantasy about your
handyman? . . . Well, it's awkward
because he is literally like, cleaning
the shit out of my toilet bowl right
now. And I don't think I'm at my
most alluring . . . Yeah, maybe you're
right. It's not like I met him socially
. . . Okay thank you Cindy. You're a
really good friend . . . OK like twenty
minutes. 'Bye!

IN HER SMALL LIVING ROOM—He comes out of the bathroom.
MARIANNE is now dressed up to go out. She looks great.

LEE

All set.

MARIANNE

Thank you so much. Can I give you a
tip?

LEE

You mean, like a suggestion?

MARIANNE
(*Taking out a ten.*)
No—I mean—like, a *tip* . . .

LEE

That's all right. Have a good night.

MARIANNE

Oh, please. I'd feel bad.

LEE

(*Takes the money.*)
OK, thanks a lot. Good night.

MARIANNE

Good night! And thank you so much.

INT. MRS OLSEN'S BATHROOM. DAY.

LEE is down on his hand and knees. MRS OLSEN, 40s, in a bathrobe, is very good-looking but bad-tempered and nervous.

MRS OLSEN

How many times do we have to fix these fucking pipes? Every time I take a shower their entire apartment has a flood. It's driving me insane.

LEE

I'll bring the plumber tomorrow but I'd say we're gonna have to break through the tile and try to isolate the leak, because there was quite a lot of water—

MRS OLSEN

But how do you know it's me? Why is it automatically me?

LEE

Because if it was coming from higher up you'd have water damage on the ceiling too, and maybe in your wall, and it's all dry.

> MRS OLSEN

Great.

LEE looks at the bathtub.

> LEE

It might just be the caulking. This whole tub needs to be re-caulked. Did you take a bath or shower in the last couple of hours?

> MRS OLSEN

Yes . . .

> LEE

Well, it could actually just be that.

> MRS OLSEN

OK. And how are you planning to find that out?

> LEE

Well, we could turn on the shower and see if it drips downstairs . . .

> MRS OLSEN

You want me to take a shower now?

> LEE

No . . .

> MRS OLSEN

You want me to take a shower while you stand there watching, to see if the water drips down into the Friedrich's apartment?

> LEE

I don't really give a fuck what you do, Mrs. Olsen. I just want to find the leak.

MRS OLSEN goes white with shock and fury.

> MRS OLSEN

No, you can get out of my apartment and don't ever come back.

LEE

OK.

MRS OLSEN *(Cont'd.)*
How dare you fucking *talk* to
me like that? Get the fuck out
of my house before I call the
police!

LEE

You're blockin' the doorway.

INT. MR EMERY'S OFFICE. NIGHT.

The building manager's office. MR EMERY is in his 50s. LEE
sits in the chair before the crowded desk.

EMERY

What the fuck's matter with you?
You can't talk to the tenants like
that!

LEE shrugs.

Look, Lee. You do a good job. You're
dependable. But I get these com-
plaints all the time. You're rude,
you're unfriendly, say you don't good
mornin'. I mean come on!

LEE

Mr Emery, I fix the plumbing. I take
out the garbage. I paint their apart-
ments. I do electrical work—which
we both know is against the law. I
show up on time, I'm workin' four
buildings and you get all the money.
So do whatever you're gonna do.

EMERY

Would you be willin' to apologize to
Mrs Olsen?

LEE

For what?

EMERY

All right, all right, I'll talk to her.

LEE gets up to go.

INT. A LOUD QUINCY BAR. NIGHT.

LEE drinks alone at a small, crowded neighborhood bar.

AT THE BAR—LEE is waiting for service. Someone bumps a CUTE GIRL, 30s, into him. She spills some beer on LEE.

GIRL	LEE
Oh my God, I'm sorry! Did I get you? Yeah. Lemme get a napkin. Lenny, could I get a couple of napkins? *(Gives LEE some napkins.)* Here you are . . .	That's OK. I'm OK . . .

                    LEE
          Thanks.
                    GIRL
          Well, now I spilled beer all over you,
          my name's Sharon.
                    LEE
          That's OK.
                    GIRL
          And you are . . .
                    LEE
          Lee.

She gets the message that he is not interested. He pats himself dry, not looking at her.

LATER—

The bar is far less packed. We see SHARON across the room, talking to a girlfriend. At the bar, LEE is drinking alone. He's pretty drunk by now. He is looking at two BUSINESSMEN, 40s. One of them notices and mentions it to the other. They look at him for a moment then ignore him. He gets up and walks toward them. They are surprised at his approach.

                    1ST BUSINESSMAN
          How you doin'?

2ND BUSINESSMAN

How you doin'?

LEE

Good. I'm good. Can I ask you guys,
have we met before?

The two men look at each other then back at LEE.

1ST BUSINESSMAN

I don't think so.

2ND BUSINESSMAN

I don't think so either.

LEE

So you guys don't know me?

1ST BUSINESSMAN	2ND BUSINESSMAN
No . . .	No, Yeah. No. Do we?
No.	

LEE

Well then what the fuck are you lookin'
at me for?

2ND BUSINESSMAN

Excuse me?

LEE

I said why the fuck are you lookin'
at me?

1ST BUSINESSMAN	2ND BUSINESSMAN
Sir, we really weren't looking	Hey! Take a fuckin' walk. Hey
at you—	—Paul—No—don't apologize
	to this asshole— *(To* LEE*)*
BARTENDER	Take a hike!
(Hurrying over.)	
Hey, Lee . . . Lee . . .!	

LEE HITS the 2ND BUSINESSMAN and knocks him into a wall.
Several pictures fall and smash on the floor.

BARTENDER

Oh, goddamnit—

LEE punches the 1ST BUSINESSMAN's nose. He falls back and

grabs his face, blood streaming from both nostrils. The 2ND
BUSINESSMAN and LEE swipe at each other.

              1ST BUSINESSMAN   2ND BUSINESSMAN
You broke my fuckin' nose!   Goddamn lunatic—

The BARTENDER leaps over the bar and grabs LEE from
behind—Other guys join in to break it up.

              BARTENDER   VARIOUS VOICES
Lee! Lee! Lee! Enough!   Break it up! Break it up!

                         LEE
         Lemme go. I gotta go take a hike.

General melee.

INT. LEE'S BASEMENT APARTMENT. NIGHT.

LEE turns the light on and comes in. He is a little roughed up
from the fight.

At his dresser, LEE pulls on sweatpants and an undershirt.
There are THREE FRAMED PHOTOS in imitation silver frames
standing on the little dresser. We don't see the photos.

LEE sits on the sofa with a beer and turns the TV on to a
late-night sports program. Slowly he falls asleep. The can in
his hand tips slowly sideways and spills onto the sofa.

EXT. LEE'S STREET. DAY.

It's snowing. Lots of slow, heavy flakes, very pretty.

EXT. LEE'S BUILDING—WINTER. DAY.

LEE is shoveling snow. The air is clear and cold. The whole
street is beautified by the recent snow storm. His iPhone
rings. He takes off his gloves. Digs out the phone.

                         LEE
              Hello . . . This is Lee . . . Oh . . . When
              did that happen? . . . Well, how is he?
              . . . OK. Uh . . . No. Don't do that. I'll
              come up right now . . . OK. Thank you.

He hangs up and goes inside with the shovel, leaving the snow before the building only partially cleared and salted down.

INT. LEE'S CAR (MOVING). DAY.

LEE sits behind the wheel, trying to get out of Boston and onto Rt 1. North. He's talking on his iPhone.

> LEE
> *(Into his iPhone.)*
> Mr Emery, it's Lee again. I contacted
> Jose, who says he can cover for me
> till Friday night at least, and then
> Gene MacAdavey can take over till
> I get back. I'll be in Manchester at
> least a week or two. I'll call again when
> I have more information. Goodbye.

He hangs up and drives into increasingly heavy traffic.

> LEE *(Cont'd.)*
> Come on, come on.

The traffic slows. He becomes increasingly anxious.

EXT. RT. 128—LEE'S CAR (MOVING). DAY.

LEE's car takes the exit for Beverly.

EXT. BEVERLY HOSPITAL. DAY.

LEE drives through the grounds of a big modern hospital. He knows exactly where he's going. He parks and gets out. He walks quickly to the main entrance, then breaks into a run.

INT. BEVERLY HOSPITAL. DAY.

We lead/follow LEE as he walks quickly through the halls toward the ICU, easily navigating the twists and turns from habit. He goes into the ICU—

INT. ICU—NURSE'S STATION—CONTINUOUS. DAY.

—and approaches GEORGE, around 50, a big weatherbeaten guy, and NURSE IRENE, 40s. They both react as LEE approaches.

> GEORGE

Hiya, Lee.

> LEE

Is he dead?

GEORGE's eyes fill with tears. He makes a helpless gesture.

> NURSE IRENE

I'm sorry, Lee. He passed away about
an hour ago.

> LEE

Oh.

> NURSE IRENE

I'm so sorry.

LEE looks at the floor, hands on his hips. NURSE IRENE gives
his arm an awkward squeeze. LEE stares into the middle
distance for a moment.

> LEE

Did you see him?

> GEORGE

Yeah. I mean—No—

> NURSE IRENE   GEORGE *(Cont'd.)*
George br—   I brought him in.

> GEORGE *(Cont'd.)*

. . . We were lookin' at the boat this
mornin', and he just—I don't know,
he just, like, fell over. I thought he
was kiddin' me at first. Then I called
the ambulance . . . and uh—that was
it.

LEE shakes his head, still staring at the floor.

> NURSE IRENE

I'll just call Dr Muller and tell him
that you're here.

> LEE

Where's Dr Betheny?

>   NURSE IRENE
> Oh, she's on maternity leave. Oh
> here he is.

DR MULLER, 40s, has just joined them.

>   DR MULLER
> Lee? I'm Dr Muller. We spoke on
> the phone.
>   LEE
> Yeah. Hi.
>   DR MULLER
> I'm very, very sorry.
>
>   LEE
> Thank you.
>   DR MULLER
> Hello, George.

He shake hands with GEORGE.

>   GEORGE
> Hiya Jim.
>   DR MULLER
> How you holding up?
>
>   GEORGE
> Oh—Great! You know.
>
>   DR MULLER
> Well . . . it's a very sad day.
>
>   GEORGE
> Yeah.

GEORGE starts to cry. He looks down and wipes his eyes.

>   LEE
> Where's my brother?
>
>   DR MULLER
> He's downstairs. You can see him if
> you want.
>   LEE
> What happened?

DR MULLER

Well, you know his heart was very
weak at this point, and it just gave
out. If it's any comfort, I don't think
he suffered very much. I'm sorry you
didn't get here in time, but as I told
you on the phone—

LEE

Aw, *fuck* this. *(He looks at the floor.
Long pause. He looks up.)* Sorry.

DR MULLER   GEORGE

That's perfectly all right.   That's OK, buddy.

LEE

Did anybody call my Uncle?

DR MULLER and GEORGE glance at each other.

GEORGE

Their Uncle Donny.

LEE   GEORGE *(Cont'd.)*

Yeah, my Aunt and Uncle.   No, Lee—Lee, no—
Somebody shoulda called
them. What?

GEORGE *(Cont'd.)*

—Donny got a job in Minnesota,
like—

LEE   GEORGE *(Cont'd.)*

Minnesota?   —awhile ago. Yeah: He got
                             job with some outfit in a
                             Minnetonka, Minnesota,
                             if you can believe that. Joe
                             didn't tell you about that?

LEE

No.

GEORGE

I can call 'em if you want, Lee. And
tell 'em what happened.

> LEE
>
> OK. Thanks . . .

LEE *(Cont'd.)*
Tell 'em . . . Tell 'em what
happened. Tell 'em I'll call 'em
tonight, probably tomorrow.
Talk about arrangements.

GEORGE
Oh, no problem—

> GEORGE *(Cont'd.)*
> Sure, I can do that.

> LEE
> And somebody better call my wife.

There is a confused, embarrassed hesitation.

> DR MULLER
> Your . . .

LEE
Ex-wife. Yes. Sorry. I meant
Randi.

GEORGE
You mean Randi? That's
OK—I already thought of
that. I'll take care of it.

> LEE
> OK, thanks.

> GEORGE
> No problem.

> LEE
> Can I see him now?

> DR MULLER
> Sure.

> GEORGE
> Lee—I can wait up here, Lee, in case
> you need anything.

> LEE
> OK.

DR MULLER leads LEE away. GEORGE breaks down again.

> GEORGE
> I'm sorry.

> NURSE IRENE

Would you like a Kleenex?

> GEORGE

Thanks. Yeah.

INT. HOSPITAL ELEVATOR.

DR MULLER and LEE ride down very slowly.

> LEE

How is Dr Betheny?

> DR MULLER

Oh, she's doing very well. She just
had twin girls.

> LEE

Oh yeah. Irene told me.

> DR MULLER

Apparently weigh about eleven
pounds apiece. So she's gonna have
her hands full for a while . . . I'll call
her this afternoon and tell her what
happened.

> LEE

She was very good to him.

> DR MULLER

Yes she was.

EIGHT YEARS AGO—

INT. JOE CHANDLER'S HOSPITAL ROOM. DAY.

JOE CHANDLER is lying in the hospital bed. There's a close
resemblance between him and Lee.

ELISE, Joe's wife, the same age as Joe, pretty, anxious and
high-strung—stands near to STANLEY CHANDLER—LEE and
JOE's father, 70s. He sits in one chair. LEE sits in another.

They are all listening to DR BETHENY, 30s. She is small,
intense, very serious and focused and level-headed, but
thoroughly well-meaning and decent.

DR BETHENY

The disease is commonly referred to
as congestive heart failure—

ELISE

Oh my *God*!

DR BETHENY

Are you familiar with it?

ELISE

No . . .!

JOE

Then what are you sayin' "Oh my
God" for?

ELISE

Because what *is* it?

JOE

She's tryin' to explain it to us, honey.
I'm sorry, Dr Beth . . . uh . . .

DR BETHENY

Betheny.

JOE	DR BETHANY *(Cont'd.)*
I'm sorry. I can never get it right.	Don't worry about it. Not a problem.

STAN

So, you were saying, Dr Beth.

JOE	LEE
It's Dr Betheny, Dad.	Dr Betheny, Daddy, try to get it right . . .

ELISE

It's a comedy routine!

JOE	STAN
Would you let her tell it?	Elise, please . . .

ELISE

Oh my God: When am I gonna put
one foot right?

JOE

Honey, for Christ's sakes!

ELISE

How about a hint?

STANLEY takes ELISE's hand and holds onto it.

STAN

Elise . . . Sweetheart . . . Let's just let
her explain the situation to us . . .

LEE

Daddy . . .

STAN

What? She's fine. We're all upset.
We're all gonna listen, then we're
gonna ask everything we wanna ask,
and then we're gonna figure out
what do to, together. Right?

JOE

Right.

DR BETHENY

It's a gradual deterioration of the
muscles of the heart. It's usually
associated with older people, but in
rarer cases it will occur in a younger
person. Some people can live as long
as fifty or sixty years with just an
occasional attack. But most people
suffer periodic episodes, like the one
you had on Monday, which mimic
the symptoms of a heart attack and
which further weaken the muscle.
They can put you out of commission
for a week, two weeks. And you'll
need to be hospitalized so we can
monitor your heart, because the risk
of cardiac arrest is elevated for a
week or two.

ELISE

Oh my God.

STAN
(Pats her hand.)
OK . . . OK . . .

DR BETHENY

But in between these episodes, most
people feel perfectly healthy and you
can basically live a normal life.

JOE

So . . . What do you mean that some
people live as long as fifty or sixty
years? You mean total? Or from when
they're diagnosed with this, or what?
And tell me the fuckin' truth.

DR BETHENY

Total.

Everyone is stunned into silence, even ELISE.

DR BETHENY *(Cont'd.)*

For approximately eighty percent of
patients your age the most common
statistical life expectancy is five years
or less.

ELISE grips STAN's hand. LEE looks at the floor.

JOE

Wow.

DR BETHENY

But the statistics vary widely, and
they're just statistics. You're not
a statistic, you're just one person,
and we don't know what's going to
happen to you yet. But it's not a
good disease.

JOE

What's a good disease?

DR BETHENY

Poison Ivy.

ELISE

(Rising.)

I do not see where the humor lies in
this situation.

STAN

Elise, you must calm down.

JOE	DR BETHENY
Honey, please . . .	I'm sorry. I'm really not trying to—

LEE

(To DR BETHENY.*)*

Don't—it's fine.

ELISE pulls her hand away from STAN and waves "No" at them.

ELISE

No. No more—I'm not gonna—

STAN	ELISE *(Cont'd.)*
Elise, let's get you a glass of water—	No m—*No.*

LEE

Daddy. Forget it.

JOE

(To LEE.*)*

Hey, shut up.

ELISE

Yeah, forget it. Forget it like you—
No, you know what? I'm tired of
bein' the bad guy here.

JOE	STAN
Jesus Christ! Who's in the fuckin' hospital?!	Nobody th—

ELISE

Right! So I'll be the bad guy, and

you be in the hospital and explain
the jokes to your son. I'm goin' home.

| JOE | STAN |
| You're goin' home. | Sweetheart— |

SHE WALKS OUT fast, her heels clicking against the floor.

STAN *(Cont'd.)*
Lemme get her back.

LEE

Fuck her.

| JOE | STAN |
| You wanna stop that shit? | Come on with that stuff already! |

THE PRESENT—

INT. HOSPITAL ELEVATOR/LOWER LEVEL HALLWAY.

The ELEVATOR DOOR OPENS AT LL2. DR MULLER and LEE
come out.

INT. MORGUE.

A SECURITY GUARD opens the door for DR MULLER and LEE.

DR MULLER
Thank you, Tony.

LEE goes in and looks down at the body. Pause.

LEE
(Hesitates.)
OK.

DR MULLER
Take your time.

LEE moves closer to the body. He touches JOE's hand. It feels
dead so he touches his shoulder where there's a sleeve. He
leans over and kisses his cheek. He embraces the body as
best he can. DR MULLER drops back discreetly. LEE walks out
past DR MULLER. DR MULLER follows.

DR MULLER *(Cont'd.)*
(To the SECURITY GUARD.*)*
Thanks, Tony.

INT. ELEVATOR.

LEE and DR MULLER ride up again in silence.

INT. BEVERLY HOSPITAL. ICU. FLOOR. DAY—CONTINUOUS.

The ELEVATOR DOOR OPENS. LEE and DR MULLER come
out and walk to the Nurse's Station, where IRENE and
GEORGE wait.

LEE
I gotta get up to Manchester. Nobody
told Patrick, right?

DR MULLER
No—you had asked us to wait for you
to get here—

LEE
(On "us".)
Yes—Thank you. So . . . What is the
procedure now?

DR MULLER
Well—You should make arrangements with a funeral parlor, and they
pretty much take care of everything.

LEE
I don't know the name of one.

DR MULLER
We can help you with that.

NURSE IRENE
Yeah.

LEE
And they come up and get him?

DR MULLER
Yes.

> NURSE IRENE

Yes.

> GEORGE

I'll make those calls, Lee—

GEORGE *(Cont'd.)*	LEE
Lemme know if you need any help with anything.	OK. And—OK. Thanks. And—Yeah. Plus I gotta call you about the boat, and the web site. All that shit.

> GEORGE

Sure. I'm around.

> LEE

OK. I better get up there before school lets out.

> DR MULLER

You just have to sign for Joe's belongings.

NURSE IRENE takes LEE around to the nurse's station so LEE can sign for JOE's belongings.

SEVEN YEARS AGO—

EXT. THE SEA—JOE'S BOAT. DAY.

Autumn. LEE, JOE and 8-YEAR-OLD PATRICK are on JOE's BOAT. The Cape Ann coast is in the distance. The boat is rigged for whale-watching and deep sea fishing charters. LEE discreetly keeps a hand near the rod as 8-YEAR-OLD PATRICK trolls. JOE is at the tiller. He's looking thinner but better.

> 8-YEAR-OLD PATRICK

Like that?

> LEE

Yeah, only keep your thumb off the line, 'cause if you get a strike it's gonna slice it right open. And you know what happens then.

                    8-YEAR-OLD PATRICK
What?
                           LEE
The sharks are gonna smell that
blood and rip this boat apart.

                    8-YEAR-OLD PATRICK
No they won't. Dad, will they?

                           JOE
Oh yeah. I seen a school of sharks
tear a boat to pieces like it was made
of cardboard, just 'cause some kid
threw a band-aid in the water.

                    8-YEAR-OLD PATRICK
No you didn't.
                           LEE
Sometimes the only way to keep 'em
off is to throw the kid directly in the
ocean to distract 'em.

                    8-YEAR-OLD PATRICK
Shut up. Sharks don't even swim in
schools.
                           JOE
Is this kid smart or what?

                           LEE
Yep. And a really smart kid is exactly
the kind of quality meal a humon-
gous school of sharks is lookin' for
when they're circlin' a boat.

                    8-YEAR-OLD PATRICK
Uncle *Lee*! Shut *up*!

PATRICK's REEL starts SPINNING OUT with a thrilling whine.

           LEE   JOE
Strike! Strike!   Look out, look out!
Ease up on the drag—   You got a strike!
And watch that fuckin' thumb! Ease up, ease up!

8-YEAR-OLD PATRICK
(Hits him.)
No swearing!

PATRICK loses his balance. LEE catches him and props him up.

LEE	JOE
Don't hit *me*—! Catch the fish! We're doin' fine. *(To* JOE.*)* Just drive the boat. Patty, pull up sharp! Come on, buddy! There you go! *(To* JOE.*)* Mind your business!	What are you guys doin'? Hook the fish! Get the hook in him before he—! I'm drivin' the goddamn boat. Get that hook in him!

LEE helps PATRICK pull the rod back sharply a few times.

8-YEAR-OLD PATRICK
What kind of fish is it?

JOE	LEE
Gotta be a great white, Patty —Maybe a barracuda—	Feels like a great white shark to me.

8-YEAR-OLD PATRICK
SHUT UP!

PATRICK is ecstatic with nerves and excitement.

THE PRESENT—

INT./EXT. LEE'S CAR (MOVING)/RT. 128 NORTH. DAY.

LEE drives up the highway.

EXT. THE OCEAN—MANCHESTER-BY-THE-SEA. DAY.

FROM THE OCEAN—We see the wealthy summer resort clinging to the Cape Ann winter coastline.

INT. LEE'S CAR (MOVING) DAY.

Thru the windshield, LEE sees the MANCHESTER EXIT approach. He takes the exit.

INT./EXT. LEE'S CAR/MANCHESTER. DAY.

LEE drives past the old houses of the little town.

SEVEN YEARS AGO—

INT. LEE'S MANCHESTER HOUSE. DAY.

Evening of the same day as the fishing scene. LEE comes into his small house and takes off his wet things. In the living room, his daughter SUZY, 7, is watching TV. A fire is crackling behind a fire screen. A radio is playing O.S.

> RANDI *(O.S.)*
> Hello?

> LEE
> Hi honey! *(To the girl.)* Hi, Suzy.
> Daddy's home. *(Pause.)* Hi, Suzy.
> Daddy's home.

> SUZY
> Hi Daddy.

> LEE
> Hi, sweetheart.

He bends down to kiss her. She hooks her arm around his neck and pulls him off balance, her eyes locked on the TV screen.

SUZY	LEE *(Cont'd.)*
Hug.	Jesus Christ, you're breakin' my neck.

He kisses her and she releases him.

> RANDI *(O.S.)*
> Lee?

> LEE
> Yeah, hiya!

INT. BEDROOM. DAY.

RANDI, LEE's wife, 30s, is in bed with a cold. She is tough, loving and sarcastic. The room is littered with Kleenex and cold remedies and clothes. KAREN, 5, is playing with colored plastic blocks on the floor. There is a CRIB in a corner.

> LEE
> Hi honey.

                    RANDI
You have a good time?

                    LEE
Yeah, really good. Where's your
mother?

                    RANDI
They just left.

                    LEE
Oh *no*.

                    RANDI
Yeah, she really missed you.

                    LEE
There's always next time. Did you
sleep?

                    RANDI
Oh, yeah. It's always restful when
my mother's here.

                    LEE
That's too bad. Hi Kary.

                    KAREN
Hi Daddy.

                    LEE
          (Picking her up.)
Hello sweetheart.

                    KAREN
Put me down.

                    LEE
I'm puttin' you down. Relax.

He kisses her and starts to put her down. She wriggles and
jerks unexpectedly backward. LEE almost loses his grip.

        LEE *(Cont'd.)*   RANDI
Hey, hey, hey!   Karen . . .!

LEE
(Putting her down.)
Honey, don't jerk around like that,
I almost dropped you on your head.

KAREN
I'm making a hair salon.

LEE
Oh yeah? It's really good. You wanna
cut my hair?

KAREN
It's just for girls. I'm sorry.

LEE
I understand. *(To* RANDI.*)* How you
feelin'?

RANDI
Little better.

LEE
You sound better.

RANDI
Did you actually use the fishin'
tackle?

LEE
Yeah, we really did. Patrick got a hu-
mongous bluefish. Eighteen pounds.

RANDI
Oh yeah? That's awesome!

LEE
I never seen anybody so happy in my
life.

He crosses to her through the tissue-strewn, cluttered room.

LEE *(Cont'd.)*
It's nice in here. You keep it nice.
What a homemaker.

RANDI

Fuck off.

He tries to kiss her. She turns her head.

RANDI *(Cont'd.)*

Get away from me.

They kiss. She claps his hand onto her breast.

RANDI *(Cont'd.)*

No, don't, stop, I'm sick.

They kiss some more. She shoves him away.

RANDI *(Cont'd.)*

OK, get offa me.

LEE goes to the CRIB. Inside is STANLEY, 8 months old, awake and placid, waving his limbs at a multicolored mobile.

LEE

Hi Stanny. How come you're not cryin'?

RANDI

Let him alone. He's been quiet for half an hour.

LEE picks the baby up.

LEE	RANDI *(Cont'd.)*
Half an hour. What is that about? Take it easy. *(To the baby.)* Hiya buddy. You are very handsome.	Oh Lee, please don't pick him up!
	If he's not makin' any noise, leave well enough alone.

LEE

"Leave well enough alone." That's what me and Mummy shoulda done instead of gettin' married.

RANDI

(Opens her magazine.)

Just shut up.

LEE

... but then you wouldn't be here.
And neither would your sisters. And
I could watch the football game in my
own livin' room. That's right, I could.

RANDI

Go fuck yourself.

LEE kisses the baby and puts him back in the crib.

LEE

See? I didn't make him cry. 'Cause
I know how to handle him.

RANDI

How was Joe?

LEE

He's all right. You know? He's doin'
all right.

RANDI

And you didn't run outta beer? You
got through the day OK?

LEE

Oh yeah. We were very temperate.

RANDI

I don't know why you guys bother
gettin' on the friggin' boat.

LEE

Because we love the sea.

LEE *(Cont'd.)*

I only had eight beers over a seven
hour period. That's approximately
one point four two somethin' beers
per hour.

RANDI

No, it's almost like a normal person
stayin' sober.

> LEE
>
> I told you I was cuttin' down.

LEE starts to get undressed.

> RANDI
>
> What do you think you're gonna do?

> LEE
>
> I guess I'm gonna take a shower.
> Randi, I swear to God. You shoulda
> seen the look on Patty's face when he
> caught that fish. It was like takin'
> Suzy on the merry-go-round. It was
> like—pure happiness.

She smiles at him. LEE crawls across the bed.

> RANDI
>
> Get away. I'm sick. I'm deeply sick.

They kiss. KAREN plays on the floor. The baby waves his
arms. The TV can be heard from the other room.

> LEE *(V.O.)*
>
> He's not at school?

THE PRESENT—

EXT./INT. MANCHESTER—PINE STREET/LEE'S CAR. DAY.

LEE drives into town, talking on his cell phone.

> LEE
>
> I thought school let out at
> three o'clock—What? I'm
> sorry. My cell phone—what?

> PAUL *(O.S.)*
>
> I'm pretty sure he—
> I'm pretty sure he woulda—
> That's all right. I'm pretty
> sure he woulda left for
> hockey practice by now.

EXT. MANCHESTER ESSEX REGIONAL HIGH SCHOOL. DAY

Over an establishing shot of the big school building we hear:

LEE *(O.S.)*
He's on the hockey team?

INT. VICE PRINCIPAL'S OFFICE. DAY—CONTINUOUS.

PAUL, the vice principal, 40, is on the phone. His ASSISTANT, 50s, is on her computer nearby. WE CUT BETWEEN PAUL AND LEE.

PAUL
Yeah, he's doin' real well, too. How's Joe doin'? He gonna be OK?

LEE
He's fine. Where's the practice at? The school?

PAUL
No—It's in Gloucester.

PAUL *(Cont'd.)*	LEE
It's at the Gloucester— That's OK. Can you hear me?	It's not at school? What? I'm sorry—This phone is— Yes.
We play with the Rockport team. But they're the lead team.	I understand—

LEE
Yes. I understand—

LEE
OK, thanks, Paul. I gotta go.

PAUL
Sure thing. Give Joe my regards, will you?

LEE
I will.

INT. VICE PRINCIPAL'S OFFICE—CONTINUOUS.

PAUL hangs up.

PAUL

Joe Chandler's in the hospital again.

ASSISTANT

Oh my gosh . . . Oh my gosh. That
poor man has had more trouble . . .

PAUL

Yep.

ASSISTANT

Who was on the phone?

PAUL

That was Lee Chandler.

ASSISTANT

Lee Chandler?

PAUL

The very one.

INT./EXT. LEE'S CAR/RT 128 NORTH. DAY.

LEE drives. The SIGN for GLOUCESTER and ROCKPORT is up
ahead.

INT. GLOUCESTER MIDDLE SCHOOL—HOCKEY RINK. DAY.

The Rockport/Manchester team is having practice. PATRICK
is on the ice. He is just 16, skinny, athletic, long-haired. He is
bright, practical, pugnacious. The HOCKEY COACH, 40s, is
shouting instructions. PATRICK checks another KID against
the boards. They start fighting. They're evenly matched but
PATRICK is kind of wild. The COACH yanks PATRICK off the
other kid.

HOCKEY COACH

OK, break it up! Break it up! You!
Chandler! One more time and you
are OUT. Understand me?

PATRICK sees LEE in the stands, over the coach's shoulder..

PATRICK

Aw, fuck me.

> HOCKEY COACH
> What's that, Chandler?

> PATRICK
> Aw, fuck my fuckin' ass.

> HOCKEY COACH
> OK, you are *out*! You're *benched*!

> PATRICK
> *(To himself, skating away.)*
> Ask me if I give a shit.

> HOCKEY COACH
> What's that? What's the matter?

PATRICK skates over to LEE. The COACH sees LEE and hesitates. A small scrappy kid named JOEL skates up, followed by CJ, a big handsome athletic kid. These are PATRICK's friends.

> JOEL
> That's his uncle.

> CJ
> His dad must be in the hospital.

> HOCKEY COACH
> Whose dad? Chandler's?

> CJ   JOEL
> He's got congestive heart   . . . He only comes up when
> failure. Patrick's dad,   Mr Chandler's in the hospital.
> I mean. Not Patrick.

Some other kids skate up and are watching PATRICK and LEE.

> HOCKEY COACH
> That's Lee Chandler? *The* Lee
> Chandler?

> CJ
> Yeah, but you know that stuff about
> him's bullshit, Mr Howard.

> JOEL
> Yeah, that story's bullshit.

HOCKEY COACH
You guys wanna watch the language?

JOEL   CJ
Sorry.   Sorry.

Across the rink, LEE is talking to PATRICK. PATRICK is kicking up little shards of ice with his skate. The COACH notices that all the kids have stopped to watch.

HOCKEY COACH
OK, Everybody wanna mind their
own business? Five minute break.
That means five!

The kids break up, marginally. The COACH skates over to LEE and PATRICK. They talk briefly. The COACH puts a well-meant but sentimental hand on PATRICK's shoulder. LEE goes back up the aisle.

CJ and JOEL skate over to PATRICK. He tells them. They react sincerely and with sympathy. They squeeze his shoulder, they each hug him. All the kids are watching again by now.

HOCKEY COACH *(Cont'd.)*
OK, show's over! Let's line it up
again! Come on, line up!

The kids start skating around, lining up at the blue line. PATRICK breaks away and skates toward the exit by himself.

INT. LEE'S CAR (MOVING). DUSK.

The winter sun is getting low. PATRICK sports a semi-grunge garage-band look. Longish greasy hair, Army jacket, black T- shirt with some design on it, cargo pants maybe.

PATRICK
Oh well.

They pass a sign for MANCHESTER, BEVERLY and NORTH SALEM.

LEE
I gotta go back to the hospital and sign
some papers. Do you wanna see him?

> PATRICK
> Him who? See who?

> LEE
> Your dad. Do you wanna look at him?

> PATRICK
> I don't know. What does he look like?

> LEE
> He looks like he's dead. *(Pause.)* I
> mean, he doesn't look like he's asleep,
> or anything like that. He doesn't look
> gross . . . *(Pause.)* You don't have to.
> I wanted to see him. Maybe you don't
> want that image in your memory.
> I don't know. It's up to you.

PATRICK is silent.

INT/EXT. LEE'S CAR/HOSPITAL PARKING LOT. DUSK.

LEE pulls into a parking space. He looks at PATRICK, who is
looking slightly queasy.

> LEE
> What do you think? Should I take you
> home? Do you want me to decide?

> PATRICK
> Let's just go.

At the same instant PATRICK opens his door to step out and
LEE starts DRIVING. He slams on the brakes.

> LEE
> What the fuck are you doing?

> PATRICK
> I just said let's go inside!

> LEE
> No, you just said "Let's just go!"

LEE *(Cont'd.)*
And then you get out of the
car without telling me?
What the fuck's the matter
with you?

I coulda ripped your fuckin'
leg off, that's my problem.

PATRICK
Yeah, I meant let's go
inside. I meant let's just
go *look* at him!

OK, OK! What's your
problem?

OK! I'm sorry I misused
the English language!

They get out of the car, both more subdued.

PATRICK *(Cont'd.)*
I'm sorry, Uncle Lee.

LEE
I'm sorry too. I just got scared.

INT. HOSPITAL MORGUE.

NURSE IRENE and LEE stand by while PATRICK looks at JOE.

PATRICK
OK. Thank you.

NURSE IRENE
Of *course* . . .

PATRICK walks away. LEE and DR MULLER follow.

INT/EXT. LEE'S CAR (MOVING)/R 128 NORTH. DUSK/NIGHT.

They drive in silence.

PATRICK
Well, that was a mistake.

LEE
I guess I gave you bad advice.

PATRICK
No . . . *I* decided . . .

EXT. THE SEA. DUSK/NIGHT.

WIDE ON THE COAST: A few headlights move through in the dark town.

EXT. MANCHESTER—STREETS. NIGHT.

LEE's car drives through the narrow hilly streets.

INT. LEE'S CAR. (MOVING) DUSK/NIGHT. SIMULTANEOUS.

They drive in silence. LEE slows the car to a halt. The narrow street is blocked by an SUV by a big house. A visiting family is saying goodnight to a family in front of the house.

> LEE
> Come on . . . *(Pause.)* Come on, come on!

He HONKS the HORN LOUD, TWICE. Everybody looks at him. The CAR DAD comes around to the driver's side of the SUV . . .

> CAR DAD
> Sorry! Sorry! Come on, guys . . . !

The others continue saying goodbye and chatting. LEE HONKS the HORN several times.

LEE	PATRICK
Either get in the car or move it in the driveway!	What's the matter with you?

The CAR DAD turns around. The HOUSE DAD takes a step forward.

> CAR DAD
> What's your problem, pal?

LEE	CAR MOM
Don't tell me to relax. You're sitting in the middle of the street. (HONKS.)	We're leavin', we're leavin'! Sorry! *(Kisses* HOUSE MOM.*)* I'll call you tomorrow. *(To* LEE.*)* OK, OK, OK! In the car, kids!

PATRICK	
Would you stop it, Uncle Lee? It's the Galvins and the Doherties! Jesus!	

	CAR DAD
	You wanna play tough guy with me in front of all my kids?

LEE

Oh. It is?

PATRICK

Yes! What's the matter with you?

LEE

I'm sorry.

PATRICK
(Waving out the window.)
Hiya Mr Doherty. It's Patrick Chandler. Hi Mrs Doherty . . . Mr Doherty! It's OK: It's Patrick Chandler!

Yeah, it's just me. Hi. Sorry about that. We're just late. How are you?

PATRICK

Hi Mrs. Galvin. Hiya Mrs Doherty.

I'm OK. How are you? Sorry about that.

HOUSE MOM

Goodnight kids! Come over any time!

CAR KIDS

Goodbye! Thank you!

CAR MOM

Tommy, come on.

CAR DAD

Patrick? Is that you?

Well, for Christ's sakes! Where's the fire?

HOUSE MOM

Hello, Patrick.

HOUSE DAD

Patrick? Jesus, what's the ruckus all about? How are you?

CAR MOM

Oh for goodness sake . . . !

CAR DAD
(Squinting.)
Who is that?

PATRICK

It's just my Uncle Lee. It's my uncle.

LEE

It's Lee Chandler.

CAR DAD

Lee?

There is instant awkwardness between them.

LEE
Hi Tom. Sorry—I'm sorry: I didn't know you . . .

CAR DAD *(Cont'd.)*
Oh. Hey, Lee . . . What's all the rumpus for?

Well, keep your shirt on . . .! I'm movin'.

CAR MOM
Hello, Patrick.

PATRICK
Hi, Mrs Galvin.

LEE calls to the HOUSE DAD through PATRICK's open window.

LEE
Hello, Jeff. Hello, Arlene.

HOUSE KIDS
Hi, Patrick! Hey, Patrick!

HOUSE DAD
(Coldly.) Hey, Lee.

PATRICK
Hey guys. How's it goin'?

CU: HOUSE MOM. She pointedly refuses to answer LEE at all.

LEE
. . . Sorry about the ruckus.

HOUSE MOM
Patrick, how's your dad?

PATRICK
He's fine.

EXT. JOE'S HOUSE. NIGHT.

The car stops in front of the GARAGE of a small well-kept old clapboard house with lots of bare trees and shrubs around.

PATRICK
You gotta hit the bleeper.

LEE
I don't have the bleeper.

PATRICK
I'll do it. There's a code.

PATRICK gets out and goes to open the garage door manually.

INT. JOE'S HOUSE. NIGHT.

LEE and PATRICK come in and turn on the lights. The house is
just as it was that morning. The *Boston Globe* sports section
is spread on the sofa. One of JOE's plaid shirts is draped over
the back of the chair.

> PATRICK
>
> Is it OK if some of my friends come
> over? I told 'em I would call 'em.

> LEE
>
> Go ahead.

> PATRICK
>
> Can we get some pizza? There's
> nothing to eat here.

> LEE
>
> Yeah. Sure. *(Takes out his iPhone.)*
> What kind do you want?

> PATRICK
>
> Any kind is fine. Thank you.

LEE takes out his phone. PATRICK starts to text his friends.

INT. JOE'S HOUSE—LIVING ROOM. NIGHT.

PATRICK, JOEL and CJ and SILVIE, who seems to be PATRICK's
girlfriend, are all sitting around in the living room. They are
a bit awkward but well-meaning—except SILVIE, who is over-
relaxed and too touchy-feely with PATRICK.

> SILVIE
>
> At least he didn't suffer. It's worse
> for the family, but it's better for the
> person.

> CJ
>
> Well, he was a fuckin' great guy,
> Patrick, I'll tell you that.

> JOEL
>
> That's for sure.

                        CJ
        I remember one time he took us all
        out in the boat? Like in sixth grade?

            JOEL   CJ
I remember that.   And he made us wear life
                             preservers? And I was like,
                             "What's the difference, Mr
                             Chandler? Boat sinks in this
I remember. And he says—   weather we're dead anyway."

                                  CJ *(Cont'd.)*
                             And he says "The life jacket's
                             to make it easier on the
                             sharks when you go over."
The boys laugh.

                      PATRICK
        Yeah, he really liked those shark
        jokes.

                       JOEL
        He was funny, boy.

                      SILVIE
        Yeah, but he was gentle too, you
        know? *(Strokes* PATRICK*'s hair.)* Like
        his son.

This piece of sentimentality embarrasses everyone but SILVIE.

INT. JOE'S KITCHEN. SIMULTANEOUS.

LEE is at the table, halfway through a piece of pizza and
a beer. He finishes the beer, gets another and heads into—

INT. JOE'S LIVING ROOM. CONTINUOUS.

LEE moves through the room toward the staircase.

            CJ   JOEL
And there's this former   *Star Trek* sucks.
starship captain—this former
starship captain, shut up—   *Star Trek* sucks my ass.

SILVIE

How you doin', baby?

PATRICK

OK.

CJ *(Cont'd.)*

No it's not! Ask Patrick!
Ask him! Moron!

CJ

Star Trek is one of the pillars
of modern entertainment.

JOEL

One of the pillars of modern
entertainment is retarded.

JOEL

Read my lips. *Star Trek* is
retarded. It's retarded.

SILVIE

I can't believe we're talking about
Star Trek right now!!

This effectively kills the conversation. She goes back to
stroking his hair. LEE keeps going up the stairs.

PATRICK

I like *Star Trek* . . .

INT. JOE'S ROOM. NIGHT.

LEE snaps on the lights and comes in. The room is tidy except
for a few items: A coffee mug, an open book on the floor by
the bed. LEE opens the bottom dresser drawer and takes out
a pair of JOE's neatly folded pajamas.

INT. GUEST/LEE'S ROOM. NIGHT.

LEE lies on top of the bed, wearing JOE's pajamas, drinking
beer and watching television. PATRICK knocks and comes in.

PATRICK

Hey, Uncle Lee? Is it OK if Silvie
sleeps over? Dad always let her.

LEE

Then what are you asking me for?

PATRICK

No reason. Thanks. *(Pause.)* So—Not
that it would come up, but her parents

think she stays downstairs when she
stays over? So if it comes up for some
reason, can you just say she stayed in
the downstairs room?

> LEE
>
> I don't even know them.

> PATRICK
>
> Yes you do. It's the McGanns. Frank
> and Pat McGann.

> LEE
>
> That's Silvie McGann?

> PATRICK
>
> Yeah. So do you mind sayin' she
> stayed downstairs? Like if they call
> or something?

> LEE

OK.

PATRICK hesitates.

> LEE *(Cont'd.)*
>
> Am I supposed to tell you to use a
> condom?

> PATRICK
>
> No . . . I mean—Unless you really
> feel like it.

> LEE
>
> Is that what Joe would say?

> PATRICK
>
> No. I mean, yes. I mean, we've had
> "The Discussion" and everything.

> LEE

OK.

> PATRICK
>
> Just lemme know if we're makin' too
> much noise.

                    LEE

OK.

                    PATRICK

Hey. Do you think I should call my
mom? To tell her about Dad?

                    LEE
          (Tenses.)
I wouldn't, Patty. I don't think anybody even knows where she is . . .

                    PATRICK

All right. I was just curious what you
thought. Anyway . . . Good night,
Uncle Lee.

                    LEE

Good night.

PATRICK surprises LEE by going to him and giving him an
awkward hug. PATRICK heads for the door.

INT. GUEST/LEE'S ROOM. NIGHT.

LEE lies on the bed.

SIX YEARS AGO—

INT. JOE & ELISE'S HOUSE. SUMMER—DUSK.

The room is DARK except for the TV. Two little DOGS
start BARKING. JOE, 9-YEAR-OLD PATRICK and LEE come in
the house. They are muddy and dusty from playing softball.
They drop the softball gear, start taking off their muddy
sneakers, etc.

                    JOE
          —and now you're gonna sulk all
          night because you dropped the
          goddamn ball?

9-YEAR-OLD PATRICK   LEE *(To JOE.)*
I'm not sulking.   Why don't you stop already?
                          You wanna stop?

JOE *(To* LEE.*)*

Shut up! *(To* PATRICK.*)* If you would use a goddamn *baseball* mitt you wouldn't *drop* the fuckin' ball.

Shaddup, shaddUP, you stupid dogs! ELISE!

LEE *(To* JOE.*)*

Why don't you kill him? I think you should kill him.

9-YEAR-OLD PATRICK

I don't need a baseball mitt. I catch better without one!

JOE flicks on the LIGHTS. The small living room is trashed.

JOE

Ah, shit.

9-YEAR-OLD PATRICK

Dad! No cursing!

ELISE is PASSED OUT on the SOFA, her short nightie scrunched up underneath her. She's got no underwear on, so the men and 9-YEAR-OLD PATRICK can see everything. There's a half-empty bottle and a glass of liquor on the coffee table. Cigarette butts spill over the ashtray. JOE takes immediate control.

JOE

Lee, you wanna take Patty upstairs and get him washed up? Go on up, Patty. Everything's OK.

LEE

Come on, buddy.

POV LEE as he takes PATRICK upstairs: JOE pulls down ELISE's nightie. Looks at his shoe. There's a little dog shit on it.

JOE

Oh, come on.

POV LEE as JOE sees that the dogs have peed and crapped all over the floor—a whole day's worth.

THE PRESENT—
INT. GUEST/LEE'S ROOM. NIGHT.

LEE is lying in bed. He switches off the light. We can hear the ocean outside.

INT. PATRICK'S ROOM. SIMULTANEOUS.

SILVIE is asleep on PATRICK's single bed. PATRICK is at his desk typing on his laptop. We see what he is TYPING:

"Dear Mom—"

EXT. JOE'S HOUSE. DAY.

A clear cold day. The house has a nice view of the town.

INT. KITCHEN. DAY.

LEE is dressed and seated at the table with a cup of coffee, talking on his iPhone.

> LEE
> *(On the phone.)*
> Beverly, Massachusetts . . .
> Gallagher Funeral Home please . . .

SILVIE comes through the kitchen door, dressed, very comfortable in the house.

> SILVIE
> Morning.

> LEE
> Hello.

Over the following she gets some juice and yogurt out of the fridge, some herbal tea, and puts on the kettle, while LEE watches her. PATRICK enters, gets some cold cereal.

LATER—They are all at the table. LEE is still on the phone.

> PATRICK
> Pass the milk please.

> LEE
> So but, I don't know what I gotta do

to get his body from the hospital to
your place, but they said . . . Oh,
OK . . .

SILVIE

Excuse me, Mr Chandler? I don't
think Patrick needs to be here for
this.

PATRICK

That's all right.

LEE gets up and goes out. SILVIE puts a hand on PATRICK's
hand. We can hear LEE'S VOICE from the other room.

LEE *(O.S.)*

So why is it more to drive his body to
Manchester? 'Cause you gotta take
the highway for seven minutes?
What do you charge if the hearse
takes 127?

SILVIE

Jesus. Like that's his focus?

PATRICK

He's alright.

EXT. MANCHESTER ESSEX REGIONAL HIGH SCHOOL—
HALL. DAY.

LEE's car stops in front of the school gate. PATRICK and SILVIE
climb out from the back.

PATRICK   SILVIE
Thanks, Uncle Lee.   Thanks a lot, Mr Chandler.

He watches them walk toward the school, joining a general
swarm of kids funneling to the school entrance.

INT. SCHOOL. DAY.

PATRICK walks thru the halls. Various kids greet him with ex-
pressions of sympathy.

> KID'S VOICE
> Hey, Patrick. Sorry to hear about
> your dad, man.

> PATRICK
> Oh—Thanks, man. Thank you.

He presses thru. Other kids stop him with condolences.

INT. ATHLETIC DEPARTMENT OFFICE. DAY.

HOCKEY COACH Mr. Howard is seated. PATRICK stands.

> HOCKEY COACH
> We're gonna forget about the
> language. We're gonna forget about
> the fists. But I want you to take a
> few days offa practice. I don't want
> you on the ice. You got enough on
> your mind.

> PATRICK
> That's OK, Mr Howard. To tell
> you the truth, I could use the
> distraction—

> HOCKEY COACH
> The ice is not a distraction. When
> you're on the ice, you gotta be there.
> Take the week and we'll talk. And
> listen: I lost my dad right about your
> age. So I know what you're goin'
> through. So if you wanna come in
> and talk, or you just want somebody
> to spill your guts to—or you just wanna
> throw the bull around, door's open.

INT./EXT. LEE'S CAR/MANCHESTER ESSEX HIGH SCHOOL.
DAY.

LEE picks PATRICK up from school and they drive away.

INT. LEE'S CAR (MOVING) DAY.

They drive through town.

> PATRICK
> You mind if I put some music on?

> LEE
> No.

PATRICK turns the radio to some pop-rock station.

> PATRICK
> You like these guys? The lead guitar
> is weak but otherwise they're pretty
> good.

> LEE
> They all sound the same to me.

> PATRICK
> Where we going?

> LEE
> To see the lawyer.

> PATRICK
> What for?

> LEE
> We gotta read your father's will.

> PATRICK
> Can't you just drop me at home and
> tell me what it says in it?

> LEE
> Well, yeah—except we're there.

They are approaching the Manchester's tiny business
district.

EXT. STREET—LAWYER'S OFFICE. DAY.

They walk toward the little two-story office building.

PATRICK
Who do you think he left the boat to?

LEE
I'm sure he left you everything.

As they go up the OUTDOOR STAIRWAY to the second-story office, We hear the SOUND of a PING-PONG game: Ka-POP, ka-POP, plus other growing sounds of voices and music. They take us to—

FIVE YEARS AGO—

INT. LEE & RANDI'S HOUSE—BASEMENT DEN. NIGHT.

LEE is playing PING-PONG with TOM DOHERTY—the CAR DAD. A bunch of his friends are drinking and making noise. Loud music. We spot JOE and GEORGE. LEE SLAMS the BALL.

LEE
Eat my fuckin' forehand, Tommy!

TOM	LEE *(Cont'd.)*
Once! That was once! He punts the ball sixteen times and now he's Superman.	I got it workin' now. Just keep away from this quadrant and you won't go home in tears.

RANDI appears at the top of the basement stairs in a bathrobe. Everybody looks up at her, like little boys.

RANDI
Would you keep it down, you fuckin' morons? My kids are sleepin'.

LEE
I'm sorry, honey. *(To* the GUYS.*)* I *told* you guys to keep it down.

RANDI	THE GUYS
Lee, you wanna get these fuckin' pinheads outta my house please?	Yeah, Sorry, Ran. I *told* you guys to keep it down.

RANDI leaves.

>   LEE
>   She can't talk that way to us.

>   TOM
>   Yeah. We're not pinheads.

EVERYBODY LAUGHS. RANDI immediately appears again, furious.

>   RANDI
>   Hey! I'm not fuckin' around! It's
>   two o'clock in the fuckin' mornin'!
>   Get these fuckin' assholes dressed
>   and get 'em the fuck outta here.

THE PRESENT—

INT. LAWYER'S OFFICE—WAITING ROOM. DAY.

PATRICK sits, texting. An ASSISTANT types at her computer.

INT. LAWYER'S OFFICE. DAY—SIMULTANEOUSLY.

WES, 40s, sits behind his desk across from LEE. Each holds a copy of Joe's will.

>   LEE
>   I don't understand.

>   WES
>   What—part are you having trouble
>   with . . .?
>   LEE
>   (On "trouble".)
>   *I* can't be Patrick's guardian.

>   WES
>   I understand it's a serious responsi-
>   bility—
>   LEE
>   No—I mean—I mean, I *can't*—

>   WES
>   Well—Naturally I assumed that Joe
>   had discussed this with you—

LEE

No. He didn't. No.

WES

Well . . . I must say I'm somewhat
taken aback—

LEE

He can't live with me:

LEE *(Cont'd.)*	WES
I live in *one room*.	But if you look—Now, well, if you look, you'll see Joe provided for Patrick's upkeep: Clothes, food, et cetera . . . The house and boat are owned outright . . .

LEE

I don't see how I could be his
guardian.

WES

Well, those were your brother's
wishes.

LEE

Yeah but I can't commute from
Boston every day until he turns
eighteen.

WES

I think the idea was that you would
relocate.

LEE	WES *(Cont'd.)*
Relocate? Where? Here?	If you look at—

WES *(Cont'd.)*

Well, yes. As you can see, your
brother worked everything out
extremely carefully.

LEE

But—He can't have meant
that.

WES *(Cont'd.)*

And if you—Well, you can see
he's allowed up to five
thousand dollars to help you
with the move. There's a
small amount set aside for you
to draw from, as personal
income while you settle in—
assuming of course that you
accept . . .

LEE

What about Uncle Donny and
Teresa?

WES

Well, they did come up. But Joe
didn't feel that Patrick really had any
special relationship or feeling about
them—

LEE

I don't understand.

Minnesota.
Minnetonka, Minnesota.

WES *(Cont'd.)*

And now, I think you know
Wisconsin, I believe . . .
they've moved out to
Minnesota, that's right. So . . .

WES watches as LEE flips through the 3-PAGE WILL as if
there's something he may have missed. After a moment:

WES *(Cont'd.)*

It was my impression you've spent a
lot of time here over the years . . .

LEE

Just as backup. I came up to stay
with Patty whenever Joe was in the
hospital, after my dad couldn't do it.
We—It was supposed to be my Uncle
Donny. I was just the backup.

> WES
>
> Well . . . I can only repeat, I'm aston-
> ished that Joe never ran all this by
> you, thorough as he was.

> LEE
>
> Yeah, because he knew what I would
> say if he would have asked.

FIVE YEARS AGO *(Cont'd.)*—

LEE stands outside waving and shouting goodbyes to the
CARS DRIVING AWAY. His friends respond with car horns
and apologies. RANDI stands inside, wrapped in a bathrobe.

LEE *(Cont'd.)*	THE GUYS
See Jupiter? Good night! Keep your eyes on the road! You see Jupiter? Keep your eyes on the road! Good night Tommy! Good night Joe! Sorry again! *(To* THE GUYS.*)* See the North Star? There's the North Star, right there!	Good night, Lee! Tell Randi we're sorry! We're so sorry! Good night, etc.

> TOM *(O.C.)*
>
> Where?

> LEE
>
> It's due north . . .!

A MOMENT LATER—LEE shuts the front door, shivering in
his shirt sleeves. He tries to kiss RANDI. She turns her head.

> LEE *(Cont'd.)*
>
> I'll clean up in the morning, baby.

> RANDI
>
> You see Jupiter you fucking asshole?

He laughs.

> LEE
>
> Come on . . .

She lets him kiss her, then she goes off toward their bedroom. LEE shivers and rubs his arms.

INT. LAWYER'S OFFICE. DAY—SIMULTANEOUS.

LEE is still staring at the will.

> WES
>
> Lee . . .

FIVE YEARS AGO *(Cont'd.)*—

EXT. MANCHESTER STREET—MINI-MART. NIGHT.

Cheerfully drunk, LEE walks along the crunchy snow-covered sidewalk and into a mini-mart. It's a very cold clear night.

THE PRESENT—

INT. LAWYER'S WAITING ROOM. DAY.

PATRICK is still texting away in the armchair.

> WES'S ASSISTANT
>
> Patrick? Can I get you a soda or anything?

> PATRICK
>
> No thank you.

FIVE YEARS AGO *(Cont'd.)*—

EXT. MINI-MART. NIGHT.

THROUGH THE WINDOW we see the clerk bag two six-packs, milk, and some Pampers for LEE. LEE comes out of the store. He has some drunken trouble zipping his parka as he heads home. He doesn't notice the orange-red GLOW in the sky ahead.

THE PRESENT—

INT. LAWYER'S OFFICE. DAY.

WES

Lee . . . Nobody can appreciate what
you've been through . . . If I can say
that. And if you really don't feel you
can take this on, that's your right,
obviously—

LEE

But who would get him?

WES

The probate court would appoint a
guardian in your place.

LEE

Like who?

LEE *(Cont'd.)*	WES
My Uncle Donny?	I don't know—No—Not necessarily. Especially, now with the distance.

LEE

Who else would there be?

WES

Well . . . I don't know what's
happening with Patrick's mother—

LEE *(Cont'd.)*	WES
No. No.	I'm not sure where she is, or what her condition is—But you can bet the judge would certainly look into it.

LEE

. . . No . . . Can't do that.

FIVE YEARS AGO *(Cont'd.)*—

EXT. LEE'S STREET. NIGHT.

LEE slows as he nears the turn to his street. He is looking at
the FIERY SKY and FLASHING LIGHTS. He starts to run—

THE PRESENT—

INT. LAWYER'S OFFICE. DAY.

LEE sits staring out Wes's window at the harbor.

>   WES
> There is Patrick to be considered.

FIVE YEARS AGO *(Cont'd.)*—

EXT. LEE & RANDI'S HOUSE. NIGHT.

The little HOUSE is COMPLETELY ON FIRE. Fire trucks
and FIREMEN are pumping water into the blinding SMOKE.
There is also an ambulance and police cars. TWO POLICEMEN
are trying to control RANDI. She's in a nightgown smeared
with smoke and water. She thrashes violently to shake them
off so she can run into the flaming house. She is completely
hysterical.

>   RANDI
> Let me go! Get your hands off me!
> Let go of me! Somebody go *in* there!
> Let me go! Get them outta there!

We PAN the faces of a clutch of neighbors looking on,
mortified, until we land on LEE staring at the blazing house.
He still holds the paper bag from the mini-mart.

>   DISSOLVE TO:

EXT. LEE'S HOUSE. DAWN.

The sky is getting light. The fire is out. The smoking house
is burnt to nothing. The neighbors have been pushed back by
the police and firemen.

TWO EMS WORKERS are putting RANDI into the ambulance.
She's on a stretcher and wears an oxygen mask. She is half
conscious.

TWO POLICEMEN are questioning LEE. He's still holding the
grocery bag. JOE is standing next to him now hastily stuffed
into his winter coat. He grips LEE's arm with a gloved hand.

The ambulance with RANDI in it drives away. LEE looks
past the policemen as EMS WORKERS approach the next
ambulance. They are bringing and loading THREE COVERED
STRETCHERS bearing THREE LITTLE BODIES into the
ambulance as LEE watches. In the last stretcher the smoke-
blackened ELBOW of a LITTLE GIRL sticks out a little from
under the blanket. An EMS WORKER quickly pushes it under
again.

They put the stretchers in the ambulance and shut the doors.
Without moving LEE starts crying hopelessly. The TWO COPS
stop trying to talk to him. JOE holds LEE's arm throughout.

THE PRESENT—

INT. LAWYER'S OFFICE. DAY.

LEE looks from the will to the view out the window.

WES	LEE
Look—Lee—	Thanks, Wes. I'll, uh, I'll be in touch.

LEE gets up abruptly and heads for the door.

FIVE YEARS AGO *(Cont'd.)*—

EXT. MANCHESTER POLICE STATION. DAY.

PUSH IN ON a weatherbeaten old building backed by the
marina.

INT. MANCHESTER POLICE STATION—MAIN OFFICE. DAY.

JOE and STAN wait for LEE at one end of the office with a
few desks and six or seven police officers going about their
business.

INT. POLICE STATION—INTERVIEW ROOM. DAY.

SLOW PUSH IN ON LEE at a table, facing a POLICE DETECTIVE,
a UNIFORMED POLICEMAN, and the STATE FIRE MARSHAL.

LEE

You know. We were partyin' pretty
hard. Beer, and somebody was passin'
around a joint. Somebody else had
some cocaine.

1ST DETECTIVE

Cocaine?

LEE

Yes.

1ST DETECTIVE

OK. Go on.

LEE

Anyway, our bedroom's in the downstairs. The girls sleep upstairs. So
Randi makes everybody leave around
two o'clock, maybe three AM, and
she went back to bed. So everybody
leaves, and I go inside. And it's really
cold inside, so I go check on the girls,
and it's fuckin' freezing up there. We
sleep downstairs. The girls sleep in
the upstairs. But Randi doesn't like
the central heat because it dries her
out her sinuses, and she gets these
headaches. So I went downstairs and
built a fire in the fireplace, and I sit
down to watch TV, except there's no
more beer. And I'm still jumpin' like
a jackrabbit. So I put a couple big
logs on the fire so the house would
warm up when I was gone, and I
went to the mini-mart . . . It's about
a fifteen minute walk both ways. But
I didn't wanna drive cause I was
really wasted. And I'm halfway there,
and I remember I didn't put the screen
back on the fireplace. But I figure it's

probably OK. So I kept going to the store. And that's it. One of the logs musta rolled out on the floor when I was gone. The girls were all upstairs . . . And that's it. The firemen got Randi out. She was passed out downstairs. And then they said the furnace blew, and they couldn't go inside again. And that's all I remember.

(Pause.)

1ST DETECTIVE

OK, Lee. That's all for now. We'll call you if anything else comes up we want to ask you about.

FIRE MARSHAL

Assumin' the forensics bear you out . . . which I'm assumin' that they will . . .

LEE

What do you mean? That's it?

FIRE MARSHAL

Look, Lee: You made a horrible mistake. Like a million other people did last night. But we don't wanna crucify you. It's not a crime to leave the screen off the fireplace.

LEE

So . . . What? I can go?

FIRE MARSHAL

Unless somethin' else comes up that we don't know about already, yeah.

1ST DETECTIVE

You got a ride back home?

LEE

Yeah.

INT. POLICE STATION—MAIN ROOM. DAY—CONTINUOUS.

LEE comes out of a room opposite, followed by the DETECTIVE and FIRE MARSHAL. He makes his way past the desks. Suddenly he GRABS a YOUNG COP from behind, pulls the GUN out of his holster and shoves him away. SHOUTS and GUNS come out everywhere. LEE puts the GUN to his own HEAD and pulls the trigger, but the SAFETY CATCH is ON. JOE is across the room in a bound.

> JOE
> Don't shoot! Don't shoot!

LEE fumbles with the safety catch—TWO COPS take him DOWN and grab the GUN. He doesn't resist at all. JOE joins the fray. STAN staggers and reaches for the wall behind him.

THE PRESENT—

INT. LAWYER'S WAITING ROOM. DAY.

LEE comes out of the lawyer's office. PATRICK gets up.

> LEE
> Alright. Let's go.

> PATRICK
> Where to, the orphanage?

> LEE
> Shut up.

> PATRICK
> What the hell did I do?

> LEE
> Just be quiet.

LEE heads for the exit. PATRICK follows him out.

EXT. OFFICE BUILDING. DAY.

LEE and PATRICK come out of the building, LEE first. They walk to the car. He digs out his keys.

LEE

All right. We got a lot to do.

PATRICK

What about the boat?

LEE

We gotta talk to George about it.
There's no point hangin' onto it if no
one's gonna use it—

PATRICK

I'm gonna use it.

LEE

It's gotta be *maintained*—

PATRICK	LEE *(Cont'd.)*
I'm maintaining it.	. . . we gotta change the rental
I'm gonna maintain it.	of the boat yard from Joe to
	me—No, you can't maintain
	it by yourself—

PATRICK

Why not?

PATRICK *(Cont'd.)*	LEE
It's my boat now, isn't it?	Because you're a minor. You
	can't take it out alone. Yeah
	—But *I'm* the trustee. I gotta
	make the payments, keep up
What does "trustee" mean?	with the inspections—
	It means I'm in charge of
	handling everything for you
Does that mean you're	until you turn eighteen—
allowed to sell it if I don't	
want you to?	I don't know. But I'd
	definitely consider it—

PATRICK

No fuckin' way!

LEE

Don't be so goddamn sure of
yourself! There's nobody to run it!
You're sixteen years old!

PATRICK

Yeah! I can get my licence *this year*!

LEE

So what? You're still a minor! You
can't run a commercial vessel by
yourself!

PATRICK

Why can't I run the boat
with George?

LEE *(Cont'd.)*

Meanwhile it's a big fuckin'
expense and I'm the one that's
gonna have to manage it and
I'm not even gonna be here!

PATRICK

Who gives a fuck where *you* are?

LEE

Patty, I swear to God I'm gonna
knock your fuckin' block off!

A BUSINESSMAN in a winter coat calls from across the street.

MANCHESTER BUSINESSMAN

Great parenting.

LEE

Mind your own fuckin' business!

PATRICK

Uncle Lee!

LEE

Mind your own business!
Shut the fuck up or I'll fuckin'
shut you up, I swear to God—

MANCHESTER BUSINESSMAN

No no, that's good parenting.

Smash him in the face. Smash
him in the face. That'll show
him.

LEE *(Cont'd.)*

I'm gonnna smash *you* in the
fuckin' face if you don't take
a walk! Mind your fuckin'
business!

PATRICK

It's OK, Mister. Thank you!
It's OK! Uncle LEE! Are you
fundamentally unsound?

LEE

Get in the fuckin' car!

LEE fumbles the keys and they fly out of his hands.

PATRICK

I can't obey your orders until you
unlock the door.

LEE

Just shut up.

EXT. MANCHESTER—MARINA. DAY—PRESENT.

LEE and PATRICK walk along the marina.

EXT/INT. MARINA—JOE'S BOAT. DAY.

LEE and PATRICK and GEORGE are looking at JOE'S BOAT. LEE
and PATRICK are not dressed warmly enough.

GEORGE

It's not like the motor's gonna die
tomorrow, but Joe said it's been
breakin' down like a son of a bitch.

PATRICK

Yeah, but we were gonna
take a look this weekend—

LEE

See—There's an allotment
of some kind—but things are
up in the air a little bit, so—

GEORGE

No, I can take care of it as far as
general maintenance is concerned . . .

PATRICK
I'm takin' care of it.

GEORGE *(Cont'd.)*
But that motor's gonna go
at some point . . .

LEE
There's no allotment for a new motor.
Unless you wanna buy it, George . . .

PATRICK
Wait a second. I'm not sellin' it—

LEE
Anyway, we're gonna be in Boston.

PATRICK
What? Since when am I supposed to be
in Boston?

(Pause.)

GEORGE
Well—Whatever you decide . . .

GEORGE *(Cont'd.)*
But it's gonna bleed you dry
just sittin' here . . .

LEE
It's not all worked out yet.
(To PATRICK.*)* Just take it easy!
We don't know what we're
doin' yet.

GEORGE
Well . . . you know he can always
stay with us, if he wants to come up
weekends.

LEE
You wanna be his guardian?

GEORGE is taken aback, embarrassed.

PATRICK
He doesn't wanna be my
guardian, for Christ's
sakes . . .! They got five kids
already. Have you seen his
house?

GEORGE
Well—we already got a
houseful . . . We're tryin'
to lose some kids at this
point . . .

LEE

No—we're just working out
logistics . . . So, I didn't know.

GEORGE *(Cont'd.)*

Yeah, we're jammed in there
pretty good. But we've always
got a sofa for him any time
he wants. He knows that.
(To PATRICK.*)* Right?

PATRICK

Jesus Christ, you wanna stop?
George. George. It's OK.
Really. You don't have to say
that. I know that.

He's welcome any time . . .

EXT. MARINA/WHARF. DAY.

LEE and PATRICK walk back along the wharf toward the
street and the car.

PATRICK

Are you brain-damaged? You can't
just ask people that . . .! You don't
wanna be my guardian, that's fine
with me.

LEE

It's not that. It's just the logistics. I
just gotta work it out. I swear.

PATRICK

How? By sendin' me to Wonkatonka
Minnesota with Uncle Donny?

LEE

Minnetonka!

PATRICK

OK, Minnetonka. Minnetonka
Minnesota. Same difference!

LEE *(Cont'd.)*

Minnetonka Minnesota. Not
Wonkatonka Minnesota.

PATRICK

What about my mother?

LEE stops walking, then starts again.

LEE

The judge wouldn't let her. Anyway,
no one knows where she is.

> PATRICK
>
> I do. She's in Connecticut. At least
> she was last year.

LEE stops walking again.

> LEE
>
> Since when do you know that?

> PATRICK
>
> She emailed me last year. So I
> emailed her back. You know, email?

> LEE
>
> Did your father know you were in
> touch with her?

> PATRICK
>
> Are you kiddin'? *(Pause.)* Could we
> walk? I'm freezin'.

They start walking again.

> LEE
>
> All I can tell you is—

> PATRICK
>
> I know, I know, she's a drunk, she's
> insane, she let the dogs shit on the
> floor.

> LEE
>
> —it's the last thing your dad ever
> woulda wanted.

> PATRICK
>
> Oh, like you suddenly care what he
> woulda wanted?

> LEE
>
> Aw, *fuck* everything.

INT./EXT. LEE'S CAR (MOVING) NEAR THE MARINA. DAY.

LEE and PATRICK are driving away from the marina.

> PATRICK
>
> Where to now?

> LEE
>
> The funeral parlor.

> PATRICK
>
> Great.

INT./EXT. LEE'S CAR (MOVING) MANCHESTER OUTSKIRTS.
DAY.

PATRICK notices they are now heading out of town.

> PATRICK
>
> Whoa, whoa, where're we goin'?

> LEE
>
> It's in Beverly.

> PATRICK
>
> There's no funeral homes in
> Manchester?

> LEE
>
> No. *(Pause.)* The *cemetery's* here . . .

> PATRICK
>
> Well, can you let me out? I'll just
> walk home.

> LEE
>
> Let's just get this done.

> PATRICK
>
> You wanna warn me if there's any
> other Surprise Death Errands we
> gotta run? Or is this gonna be it for
> today?

> LEE
>
> Yes. Sorry. This is it.

EXT. BEVERLY. DAY.

They drive through Beverly, a big coastal town of 40,000.

INT. GALLAGHER'S FUNERAL HOME. DUSK.

PATRICK looks around while LEE talks to the FUNERAL DIRECTOR.

EXT. GALLAGHER'S FUNERAL HOME. DUSK.

LEE and PATRICK walk away. The wind is punishing.

> PATRICK
>
> What is with that guy and the big
> Serious and Somber Act?

> LEE
>
> I don't know.

> PATRICK
>
> But seriously, does he not realize that
> people know he does this every single
> day?

> LEE
>
> I don't know. Who cares? *(Stops.)*
> I think I parked the other way. Sorry.

They reverse direction and start walking into the wind.

> PATRICK
>
> Why can't we bury him?

> LEE
>
> It's too cold. The ground's too hard.
> They'll bury him in the spring.

> PATRICK
>
> So what do they do with him 'til then?

> LEE
>
> They put him in a freezer.

> PATRICK
>
> Are you serious?

> LEE
>
> Yeah. That's what they do with them.
> They put 'em in a big freezer until the
> ground thaws out.

PATRICK

That really freaks me out.

LEE

It doesn't matter. It isn't him. It's just
his body. Where'd the car I park?

PATRICK

What about one of those mini-steam
shovels?

LEE

What?

PATRICK

I once saw one of those mini-steam
shovels one time in a graveyard in
New Haven. It dug a perfect little hole
in about two seconds.

LEE

I don't . . . really know how you would
get ahold of one. Or how much it
would cost—

PATRICK

Why can't we just look into it?

LEE

Anyway, I'm pretty sure you can't use
heavy equipment in the Historic
Rosedale Cemetery.

PATRICK

Why not?

LEE

Because there's a lot of important
people buried there, and their
descendants don't want a steam
shovel vibratin' over their dead
bodies. How do I know?

PATRICK

Why can't we bury him someplace else?

> LEE
>
> That's where he bought a plot. Don't ask me why. But if you wanna find someplace else to bury him, and find out how much it costs, and change all the arrangements with the mortician and the cemetery, and call up Sacred Heart and talk to Father Martin, and change the arrangements for the funeral service, be my guest. Otherwise let's just leave it. OK?

They turn onto a SIDE STREET. The wind picks up brutally.

> PATRICK
>
> I just don't like him bein' in a freezer.

> LEE
>
> Oh come on! Where's the goddamn car?

> PATRICK
>
> I don't know, but I wish you'd figure it out because I'm freezin' my ass off.

> LEE
>
> Don't you have a normal winter coat?

> PATRICK   LEE *(Cont'd.)*
>
> Yes.   Why don't you have gloves
>   with fingers on them?

Another gust of wind blows right through them.

> PATRICK   LEE *(Cont'd.)*
>
> Jesus *Christ*!   God *damn* it!

> LEE *(Cont'd.)*
>
> Oh where the fuck did I park the fuck-ing *car*?

EXT./INT. BEVERLY STREET/LEE'S CAR. DUSK.

They see the car on a long sloping street and run to it. They get in and slam the doors. LEE turns on the engine.

LEE

God *damn* it's cold!

PATRICK

Why? What's the matter with your
winter jacket?

LEE	PATRICK *(Cont'd.)*
Seriously, Patty—? It's on already!	Just turn the heat on
It's all the way a up! It takes a minute to warm up, so just relax, OK?	Well turn it up a little! It's blowin' fuckin' freezin' air on me.
Just be quiet.	What year did you buy this thing? 1928? Where's the horse that goes with this fuckin' car? Maybe he could breathe on us.

LEE

I swear to God—

PATRICK

I know. Why don't we just keep my
dad in *here* for the next three months?
We could save a fuckin' fortune.

LEE

Would you shut up about that freezer
please? You want me to have a
nervous breakdown because there's
undertakers and a funeral?

LEE *(Cont'd.)*	PATRICK
—Who *cares*?	*No* . . . I don't!

LEE holds his hand over the vent.

LEE

'K, it's gettin' warmer.

PATRICK

I got band practice. Can you drive me
home so I can get my stuff and then
take me over to my girlfriend's house?

LEE

Sure.

EXT. MANCHESTER. SANDY'S HOUSE. DUSK.

LEE pulls up in front of a small ranch house with a big front
yard. PATRICK twists around to gets his stuff from the back.

LEE

This is the same girl as who was over
at the house?

PATRICK

No. That was Silvie. This is Sandy.
But they don't know about each
other. So please don't say anything in
case it comes up.

LEE

I won't. *(Pause.)* Do you actually
have sex with these girls?

PATRICK

We don't just play computer games.

LEE

With both of them?

PATRICK

Well with Sandy's mom here it's sort
of strictly just basement business.

LEE

What does that mean?

PATRICK

It means I'm workin' on it.

PATRICK grabs his electric guitar and mini-amp from the back
seat. LEE watches him run across the lawn to the house.

INT. JOE'S HOUSE. NIGHT.

LEE comes in and snaps on the lights.

INT. KITCHEN. NIGHT.

LEE puts a slice of cold pizza in the microwave.

INT. SANDY'S HOUSE—BASEMENT. NIGHT.

PATRICK's ROCK BAND is practicing in the basement. SANDY, 17, brighter, wilder and more original than Silvie, sings lead vocals. PATRICK plays rhythm guitar, CJ plays lead, JOEL plays bass, a kid named OTTO plays drums. The boys sing backup. The name on the big drum is "STENTORIAN." They are playing an original composition.

> SANDY
> *(Singing.)*
> *"I gotta RUN! I gotta RUN, I, I, I, I,*
> *I, I, I gotta run—"*

> THE WHOLE BAND
> *"—I gotta run, I gotta run, I gotta*
> *run."*

> PATRICK
> Stop. Stop. Otto man, what are you doing?

> OTTO
> What did I do?

> PATRICK
> You're way behind, man.

> OTTO
> No, I'm not.

> JOEL
> You're a little behind, Otto.

> CJ
> Otto, you're kind of draggin' it . . .

> PATRICK
> You gotta stay with the bass.

JOEL

Come on man, just stay with me, all
right?

OTTO

All right, I'm sorry.

CJ

It's all right! You're alright. Let's just
take it again. Otto, you good?

OTTO

Yeah.

They get ready to take it again. PATRICK leans into his micro-
phone.

PATRICK

We are Stentorian.

They start playing again.

EXT. SANDY'S HOUSE. NIGHT.

LEE's car pulls up to the curb. Stentorian thuds through the
frozen earth. SANDY's mom, JILL, comes out and crosses the
lawn. She is 40, pretty and pleasant, hair in a pony tail. LEE
rolls down the window.

JILL

Hi, are you Lee? I'm Jill. Sandy's
mom. I think they're wrapping up.
Do you wanna come inside and have
a beer or something?

LEE

Oh, that's all right. Thank you.

JILL

I wanted to offer my condolences
about Joe. He was such a terrific guy.
There's not too many like him. He
was a wonderful father.

LEE

Thank you.

> JILL
>
> I was—I was gonna ask Patrick if he
> wants to stay for supper, if that's OK
> with you. You wanna join us? I made
> way too much . . .

> LEE
>
> Oh. That's all right. Thank you.
> What time should I come back?

> JILL
>
> Oh—I don't know. Nine? Nine-
> thirty? They're gonna do their home-
> work together. Supposedly. Ha ha ha.

> LEE
>
> OK. I'll come back at nine-thirty.

> JILL
>
> OK. You change your mind in the
> next ten minutes, we're right inside.

> LEE
>
> OK. Thank you.

JILL hesitates, smiles, then runs back to the house. LEE
drives off.

INT. SANDY'S ROOM. NIGHT.

PATRICK and SANDY are making out on her bed. PATRICK's
hand is halfway down the front of SANDY's complicated jeans.

SANDY	PATRICK
Hold on—Hold on.	Jesus Christ, I'm scrapin' the
Just take your hand out.	skin off my knuckles. How
	do you unbuckle this?

> SANDY
>
> Would you please take your hand
> outta my cunt?

> PATRICK
>
> OK, OK! *(Withdraws his hand.)* Ow!

SANDY wriggles out of her jeans.

> PATRICK *(Cont'd.)*
> Oh, are we taking our pants off?

> SANDY
> I'm takin' my pants off. I don't know
> what you're doing.

> PATRICK
> I'm takin' my pants off . . .

PATRICK tries to take off his pants, but one leg bunches up at his ankle. He kicks to get it off. She tries to help him.

> SANDY
> Come on! You gotta take your shoe
> off . . .!

> PATRICK
> I'm tryin'!

O.C., JILL KNOCKS on the DOOR. The kids both scramble away from each other and frantically start to dress.

> JILL *(O.C.)*
> Hey kids? Come on have some dinner!

PATRICK	SANDY
OK, thanks Jill! We'll be down in just one second. I just gotta log off . . .!	Thanks, Mom! We'll be right down!
	Would you shut up? She's not retarded.

> PATRICK
> Why are you pickin' on me?

> SANDY
> I'm not pickin' on you! You're going
> to get me in trouble.

INT. JILL'S HOUSE—LIVING ROOM. NIGHT.

JILL waits near the stairs. PATRICK and SANDY come down.

JILL

How's the math homework?

PATRICK

Very frustratin'.

JILL

Good.

PATRICK

Those algorithms are a bitch . . .

INT. JILL'S DINING AREA. NIGHT.

JILL, SANDY and PATRICK eat spaghetti.

PATRICK

Mm. This is really delicious, Jill.

JILL

Thank you, Patrick.

SANDY

Yeah, Mom, really good.

PATRICK

Is this a homemade carbonara sauce?

SANDY

Jesus, shut up.

JILL

Oh—no . . .

PATRICK

You could've fooled me.

SANDY

Jesus.

PATRICK

What?

SANDY

You're such a kiss-ass!

JILL

Sandy!

PATRICK

Why? Because I appreciate your
mother's cookin'?

INT. LEE'S CAR (MOVING) NIGHT.

LEE drives PATRICK home in silence. Then:

PATRICK	LEE
Aren't you gonna ask what	I don't want to know what
happppened.	happppened?—Guess not.

INT. JOE'S LIVING ROOM. NIGHT.

LEE is on the sofa with his iPhone and a beer, watching a
Celtics game. A PHONE RINGS. He looks around, confused.
Looks at his cell. Finally he realizes JOE'S LAND LINE is
ringing.

LEE
(Answering.)
Hello?

RANDI
(Over the phone.)
Hello . . . Lee? It's Randi. *(Pause.)*
Hello? Lee?

(Pause.)

LEE
Yeah. I'm here. Sorry. How are you?

RANDI
I'm OK. How are you?

LEE
Good.

RANDI
I was callin'—George told me about
Joe. I just wanted to call and say I'm
sorry. I hope you don't mind me callin'.

LEE
No. Thank you. I don't mind . . . How
are you?

RANDI

Not so good, right now. I guess we
shoulda seen it comin', but . . . it's
still kinda hard to believe . . .

LEE

Yeah . . .

RANDI

How's Patrick doin'? Beyond the
obvious, obviously . . .

LEE

He's OK. It's hard to tell with kids.

RANDI	LEE *(Cont'd.)*
Yeah—	He doesn't really open up
	with me. I think he's OK.
	He's got a lotta friends . . .
Well, that's good.	So . . . Yeah, it is . . .

RANDI

So, I don't know if you planned a
service yet, but I was also gonna ask
you if you wouldn't mind—I'd like to
be there, if it's OK with you.

LEE

Of course you can . . .

RANDI	LEE *(Cont'd.)*
OK. Thank you. It would	That's fine. You should come.
mean a lot to me—OK—	I'll let you know when it's
Thank you.	gonna be.

RANDI

Thank you. (Pause) So, can I ask—
How are you?

LEE

I don't know. How are you?

RANDI

You know. We're doin' pretty well.

I should probably tell you—I'm
gonna be—I'm pregnant. Actually.

LEE

Oh yeah?

RANDI

Yeah. Like—Ready to pop.

LEE	RANDI *(Cont'd.)*
Oh, I didn't know that.	I didn't know if I should tell you, but—

LEE

No, it's fine. Congratulations.

RANDI

Thank you. You would probably de-
duce it for yourself when you see me.

LEE

Yeah.

LEE is unable to stay on the phone any longer.

RANDI	LEE *(Cont'd.)*
So, are you still—	Actually, sorry—I don't mean to cut you off. I just gotta go pick up Patrick up and I'm slightly late.

RANDI

That's OK. I just wanted to make
sure it's OK if me and Josh come to
the funeral.

LEE

It's totally OK.

RANDI

OK. Thank you, Lee. God bless.

LEE

So long.

They hang up. LEE tries to keep a grip on himself.

INT. PATRICK'S ROOM. NIGHT.

PATRICK lies awake in the dark.

INT. LEE'S ROOM. NIGHT.

LEE lies on the bed watching a sports show and drinking beer.

EXT. MANCHESTER—CHURCH OF THE SACRED HEART. DAY.

A beautiful day. A lot of people are filing into the church.

INT. CHURCH. DAY.

SLO-MO (MOS). People are greeting PATRICK. LEE stands to one side. Some people greet him, some do not, some look at him covertly.

GEORGE and his wife JANINE, 50, say hi to LEE and PATRICK. Then a very pregnant RANDI gives PATRICK a big warm hug. She and her husband, JOSH, greet LEE. RANDI says a few words to LEE. JOSH shakes LEE's hand. Then they move away.

Others come through: Grown-ups and kids. DR BETHENY and her HUSBAND. GEORGE stays dutifully by LEE.

LATER—STILL SLO-MO (MOS) THE SERVICE. FATHER MARTIN reads the service. LEE sits in the front pew, with PATRICK, looking lost.

EXT. GEORGE'S HOUSE. DAY.

GEORGE's small, cramped, two-story house. Cars are stuffed into GEORGE's driveway and ranged up and down the block.

INT. GEORGE'S HOUSE. DAY.

The living room is packed with mourners, eating and drinking. *(Randi and Josh are not there.)* PATRICK is hugging SANDY and JILL. They are leaving. He keeps an eye out for SILVIE, who is across the room talking to CJ, JOEL and some other kids.

LATER—PATRICK is in an armchair, watching LEE through the press of chatting mourners. LEE holds a beer and looks lost. TOM DOHERTY appears, shakes LEE's hand and gives him a hug which LEE rigidly returns. MRS DOHERTY kisses LEE.

SILVIE appears at PATRICK's side. She gives him some soda in a plastic cup. Her eyes intrusively search his face.

> SILVIE
> You OK, baby?

> PATRICK
> I'm OK.

LATER—LEE and GEORGE are talking over the din.

> GEORGE
> So how you holdin' up?

> LEE
> What's the matter?

> GEORGE
> No—

LEE	GEORGE *(Cont'd.)*
What?	—I said "How you holdin' up?" It's a stupid question.
Um . . .	You get some food?

> LEE
> I had some cheese.

> GEORGE
> "You had some cheese." Asshole.

LEE	GEORGE *(Cont'd.)*
It's OK, George.	I'll get you something. Hey JANINE!

We see JANINE through the crowd, replenishing items at the buffet table and clearing paper plates and napkins, etc.

> LEE
> Seriously. I'm not hungry.

GEORGE	JANINE
Sure? *(To* JANINE.*)* Never mind! FORGET IT! SKIP IT! I SAID FORGET IT!	WHAT? I CAN'T HEAR A GODDAMN THING YOU'RE SAYIN'!

JANINE *(Cont'd.)*
DID LEE GET SOME FOOD?

INT. JOE'S HOUSE—KITCHEN. NIGHT.

LEE comes in and takes off his dark jacket and gets some cold chicken from the fridge. PATRICK comes in, iPhone in hand.

PATRICK
Hey, is it OK if I ask Silvie to stay over?

LEE
No.

PATRICK
What do you mean?

LEE
I don't want her in the house right now.

PATRICK
Why not? *YOU* don't have to talk to her . . .

LEE
I don't like her. You can go to her house or call one of your friends. That's it.

PATRICK is stunned.

INT. GUEST/LEE'S ROOM. NIGHT.

LEE gets ready for bed. We hear PATRICK in the hall O.C.

PATRICK *(O.C.)*
Would your mom be cool if I came there? . . . I have no idea.

LATER—PATRICK KNOCKS and comes in.

PATRICK *(Cont'd.)*
Well, I can't go there either.

LEE

Sorry about that.

PATRICK

So . . . Are you gonna stay in here . . .?

LEE

Well—Yeah. Why not?

PATRICK

I thought maybe you'd want to stay
in Dad's room.

LEE

Why? You want me to?

PATRICK

No. It's just a better room. And *he's*
not usin' it . . .

LEE

I'll stay in there. We're not gonna be
here that much longer anyway.

PATRICK

I'm not movin' to Boston, Uncle Lee.

LEE PATRICK (CONT'D)\

I don't wanna talk about that right
now. OK?

PATRICK

You said he left you money so you
could move.

LEE	PATRICK *(Cont'd.)*
Yes. But that doesn't mean I can just—	Anyway, what's in Boston? You're a *janitor*.

LEE

So what?

PATRICK

You could do that anywhere. There's
toilets and clogged-up drains all over
town.

LEE
I don't wanna talk about it!

PATRICK *(Cont'd.)*
All my friends are here. I'm on the hockey team. I'm on the basketball team. I gotta maintain our boat now. I work on George's boat two days a week. I got two girlfriends and I'm in a band. You're a janitor in Quincy. What the hell do you care where you live?

You can't maintain it—

LEE has no answer.

INT. JOE'S BEDROOM—NIGHT.

LEE puts the last of his stuff away. He goes to the window. The wind whistles outside.

10-YEAR-OLD PATRICK *(V.O.)*
Goodbye Uncle Lee!

FIVE YEARS AGO—

EXT. JOE'S HOUSE. DAY.

A few weeks after the girls' funeral. JOE waits by LEE's car, which is packed with a few boxes and a borrowed suitcase. LEE and 10-YEAR-OLD PATRICK come out, carrying cardboard boxes.

A moment later, LEE slams the trunk. PATRICK is inside.

JOE
Where you gonna be tonight?

LEE
I don't know. A motel.

JOE
What time you gonna call me?

LEE
When I get to the motel.

> JOE

If I don't hear from you by nine o'clock
I'm gonna call the cops. You understand?

> LEE

Yes. Yes.

> JOE

Patty! Come say goodbye to Uncle Lee!

> LEE

That's OK.

> JOE

It is not OK. Patrick! Come say goodbye!

> 10-YEAR-OLD PATRICK *(O.S.)*

Comin'!

They wait. JOE hugs LEE. LEE hugs him back woodenly. Then with more feeling. Then he breaks away and gets in the car.

> LEE

I'm gonna see him . . .

He starts the motor. PATRICK comes running out of the house.

> 10-YEAR-OLD PATRICK
> *(Exactly as before.)*
> Goodbye Uncle Lee!

> LEE

So long.

He drives off. JOE and PATRICK watch him drive away.

PRESENT—

INT. KITCHEN. NIGHT.

PATRICK, in his sleeping gear, opens the refrigerator, looking for a snack. He opens the overcrowded freezer and some packages of frozen chicken breasts and chopped meat slide out at him. He tries to catch or block them, but most of them get past him and hit the floor.

INT. JOE'S ROOM. NIGHT—SIMULTANEOUS.

At the window, LEE hears the clatter from downstairs.

INT. KITCHEN. NIGHT—CONTINUOUS.

PATRICK looks down at the frozen meat and starts to breathe hard. He starts to put them back in but starts to feel sick. He leans his head against the freezer door then backs away, wiping his eyes.

> PATRICK
> I don't want it. I don't want it.

LEE comes in. PATRICK can't get ahold of himself.

> LEE
> Patty—

> PATRICK *(Cont'd.)*
> Somethin's wrong with me.

> LEE
> What do you mean? Like what?

> PATRICK
> I don't know! I feel really weird! I'm havin' like a panic attack or something.

> LEE *(Cont'd.)*
> Are you sick?

> LEE *(Cont'd.)*
> What do you mean?

> PATRICK
> Could you get that shit outta the freezer? I feel really weird.

> LEE
> Get ridda what? The chicken?

> PATRICK
> Yes. I don't know.
>
> I don't know! No!

> LEE *(Cont'd.)*
> Should I take you to the hospital? Do you want me to call your friends?

PATRICK runs out of the kitchen.

INT. PATRICK'S ROOM. NIGHT.

PATRICK comes in and slams the door. Pause. LEE KNOCKS O.C.

LEE *(O.C.)*

You gonna go to bed?

PATRICK

Leave me alone.

LEE *(O.C.)*

I don't think I should let you keep
the door shut.

PATRICK

Just go away!

LEE *(O.C.)*

I will. Just open up the door.

PATRICK

Fuck you.

LEE KICKS the DOOR IN. PATRICK jumps up from his bed.

PATRICK	LEE *(Cont'd.)*
Jesus! What's your problem?	I said open up the door. Are you havin' a breakdown? Should I take you to the hospital?
No! No! No!	
No! I'm just freakin' out.	
	Fine, but I can't let you freak out with the door shut. And
Just go away!	if you're gonna freak out every time you see a frozen chicken I think maybe we should take you the hospital.
No we don't—!	I don't know anything about this.

PATRICK

—I just don't like him bein' in the
freezer!

LEE

You've expressed that very clearly.
I don't like it either. But there's
nothin' we can do about it.

>   PATRICK
>   Just get out!

>   LEE
>   No.

PATRICK	LEE *(Cont'd.)*
I'm all right, OK? I just wanna be alone.	I'm not gonna bother you I'm just gonna sit here. You can be alone as soon as you calm down.

PATRICK turns his face toward the wall. Silence.

>   PATRICK
>   I'm calmer now. Would you please get
>   out?

>   LEE
>   No.

PATRICK his face turned away. LEE sits there.

FIVE YEARS AGO—

INT. QUINCY—LEE'S BASEMENT APARTMENT. DAY.

The same basement studio we saw at the beginning, minus most of the furniture. LEE stands watching JOE inspect the room. His affect is flat, colorless. 10-YEAR-OLD PATRICK is looking through the window up to the street. People's feet walk by.

>   10-YEAR-OLD PATRICK
>   Cool!

>   JOE
>   How much are they payin' you?

>   LEE
>   Minimum wage plus the room.

>   JOE
>   Let's go get some furniture.

>   LEE
>   I got furniture.

JOE

No you don't. This doesn't count as
furniture. This is not a room. Let's
go get some furniture.

LEE

Get off my back.

JOE

Patty, come on. *(To* LEE.*)* Let's go.

INT. BOSTON DEPARTMENT STORE. DAY.

JOE stands with LEE looking at an armchair. PATRICK is
spinning around in another one.

JOE

You like that one?

LEE

I love it.

JOE

Good. Now you got an armchair.
Movin' right along. Let's go look
at lamps.

10-YEAR-OLD PATRICK

Uncle Lee, try this one!

JOE

Patty! Cut the crap. Let's go get
a lamp.

LEE

I got a lamp.

JOE

You got a light bulb. Let's go get a
lamp. Patty, come on.

INT. LEE'S BASEMENT APARTMENT. NIGHT.

JOE finishes tearing the paper off the armchair. The studio
now has almost all the same furniture as in the present. LEE
stands watching. PATRICK is playing a little computer game.

                              JOE
   Better? Better.

THE PRESENT—

INT. THE KITCHEN. DAY.

LEE and PATRICK are at the breakfast table. PATRICK is eating breakfast. LEE has coffee.

                    LEE
Listen. *(Pause.)* We can stay until your school lets out. That'll give me time to set things up in Boston better. You can do some stuff with George in the summer if you want . . . And you don't get jerked out of your life overnight.

                    PATRICK
   Are you askin' me or tellin' me?

                    LEE
   I'm tellin' you it's the best I can do.

                    PATRICK
       (On "you".)
   Then what the fuck do you care
   whether it's OK with me or not?
       (Pause.)
                    LEE
   It's half an hour away! You can come
   back here any time you want!

                    PATRICK
       From *Quincy?*

PATRICK *(Cont'd.)*

What is that, a joke? It's an hour and a half at *least*! You gotta include the other *cars*.

You couldn't get from here to Quincy in half an hour if you flew in a fuckin' *spaceship*!

LEE

Yes! No! Depending the traffic. Fifty minutes.

But we don't have to stay there! We could look in Charlestown, or Everett—

LEE *(Cont'd.)*
OK, fuck it.

INT. LEE'S CAR/MANCHESTER ESSEX REGIONAL HIGH
SCHOOL. DAY.

LEE and PATRICK pull up in front of school.

PATRICK
I need lunch money.

LEE reaches for his wallet. TWO GIRLS rap on the car window
as they pass by on their way into the building.

1ST GIRL
Hi, Patrick! Hi, Patrick!

2ND GIRL
Hi, Patrick!

1ST GIRL
Hey Patrick—!

PATRICK unrolls the window.

1ST GIRL *(Cont'd.)*
So are you goin' to *Godspell*?

PATRICK
I'm thinkin' about it.

1ST GIRL
OK, 'bye.

They move on, giggling. LEE reaches for his wallet.

LEE
Are they your girlfriends too?

PATRICK
They wish.

LEE
Doesn't George pay you a salary for
helpin' with his boat?

PATRICK
Yeah, but I'm savin' that.

                         LEE
        For what?

                       PATRICK
        New motor.

(Pause.)

He gives PATRICK $20. PATRICK gets out of the car.

                         LEE
              You goin' to *Godspell*?

INT. JOE'S BEDROOM. DUSK.

LEE puts the THREE FRAMED PHOTOS on the dresser. He
goes to the window and looks out. He BREAKS the WINDOW
with his FIST. Blood wells out of his knuckles immediately.
He hurries to the bathroom. The LAND LINE RINGS.

                      LEE *(O.C.)*
              Come on . . . !

He comes out, wrapping his hand in a towel. The blood soaks
through quickly. He picks up the phone.

                     LEE *(Cont'd.)*
              Hello?

INT. ELISE'S HOUSE. DAY—CONTINUOUS.

ELISE, dressed neatly and primly, is on the phone.

                        ELISE
                 (Over the phone.)
              Hello, is that Lee?

WE CUT BETWEEN ELISE AND LEE.

LEE freezes. He does not respond.

                    ELISE *(Cont'd.)*
                 (Over the phone.)
         Hello? Lee? It's Elise. *(Pause.)* Hello?

LEE does not respond. Blood stains the towel on his hand.

INT. JOE'S HOUSE—DINING ROOM. NIGHT.

LEE and PATRICK sit across from each other at the dinner table, eating. LEE has a bandage on his hand.

> PATRICK
>
> What happened to your hand?

> LEE
>
> I cut it.

> PATRICK
>
> Oh. For a minute there I didn't know what happened.

INT. JOE'S ROOM. NIGHT.

PATRICK comes into the room. LEE is VACUUMING up broken glass by the window. He has neatly taped a cardboard square over the broken pane. He sees PATRICK and turns off the vacuum. He throws the last scraps of cardboard and tape into a heavy duty trash bag full of broken glass, cardboard, etc.

> PATRICK
>
> Is there some reason why you didn't tell me my mom tried to call me?

LEE stops in his tracks.

> PATRICK *(Cont'd.)*
>
> She wrote me you hung up on her. She's in Essex. She wants me to see her new house and meet her fiancé. *(Pause.)* What'd you think? She couldn't get in touch with me?

> LEE
>
> I hung up because I didn't know what to say to her. And I didn't tell you 'cause I didn't know what to say to you. I'm sorry.

> PATRICK
>
> You can't stop me talkin' to her.

> LEE
>
> I don't care what you do.

He ties off the garbage bag and goes out. PATRICK follows—

INT. HALLWAY/STAIRS/LIVING ROOM/KITCHEN. CONTINUOUS.

They go down the hall, stairs, into the kitchen . . .

> PATRICK
> No, but you won't let my girlfriend come
> over and you hate my mother so much
> you won't even tell me that she called.
> You'd rather drag me back to Quincy
> and ruin my life than somebody else be
> my guardian—

> LEE
> There is nobody else.

> PATRICK
> I can live in Essex with my mom.

> LEE
> No you can't.

> PATRICK
> But if she's not an alcoholic anymore
> and she wants me to stay with her, then
> I can take the bus to my same school
> and keep all my friends, and the boat,
> and you can go back to Boston, and you
> can still—I don't know: Like, check in on
> me, or whatever, if you want to . . .

> LEE
> I can't do that.

> PATRICK
> Why?

> LEE
> I'm sorry I hung up on her. I'll call her
> back, and if she sounds semi-human to
> me, you can go have lunch with her and
> her fiancé if you want. I don't wanna
> talk about this anymore.

LEE goes out the back door with the garbage.

EXT. MARINA/WHARF. DAY.

LEE stands by as GEORGE and PATRICK pull away in JOE'S BOAT. PATRICK is driving.

INT. THE BOAT (MOVING). DAY.

> GEORGE
>
> OK! Soon as we get clear, open it up and we'll see what we can do.

> PATRICK
>
> OK!

EXT. MARINA/WHARF. DAY—CONTINUOUS.

LEE watches them go and then turns and walks away.

INT. BOAT YARD—FRONT OFFICE. DAY.

JERRY, 40s, is just coming into the front office as LEE comes thru the customer door. JERRY is immediately uncomfortable.

> JERRY
>
> Hey . . . Lee . . .! Well, what do you know?

> LEE
>
> How you doin', Jerry?

> JERRY
>
> Not bad, not too bad. I was sorry to hear about Joe.

> LEE
>
> Yeah. Thank you.

> JERRY
>
> How's Patrick doin'?

> LEE
>
> Good.

> JERRY
>
> Good. So what's goin' on?

LEE

... You know, I'm back and thinking about staying through the summer and was wondering if you had any work? If I could pick up some hours.

JERRY *(Cont'd.)*

You oughta—Sure, sure. Walter is down in Boston. He should be back tomorrow if you want to come by or ... Give him a call.

INT. BACK OFFICE—SIMULTANEOUS.

SUE, 50s, is at a cluttered desk doing paperwork. She hears voices in the front. Stops what she's doing and listens.

WE CUT BACK AND FORTH.

LEE

... Anyway, I'm just lookin' for anything right now— Fixit jobs: Boats, engines,— OK: I'll do that. No, I know. I just thought I'd ask.

JERRY

You oughta—Sure, sure. You oughta come by tomorrow and talk to Walter ... I doubt he's got anything in February—Oh, absolutely.

LEE

Thanks Jerry.

JERRY

Good to see you.

They shake hands. After LEE exits, SUE enters the FRONT OFFICE.

JERRY *(Cont'd.)*

Guess who just—

SUE

I don't wanna see him in here again.

MINI-MONTAGE—

LEE goes into 1) COASTAL AUTOMOBILE REPAIR. 2) MILNE PLUMBING & HEATING. 3) HAMMC PAINTING & REMODELING. He talks to managers, fills out forms, walks in and out of doors ...

EXT. GEORGE'S HOUSE. NIGHT.

LEE is picking PATRICK up from GEORGE's house. GEORGE and JANINE and their FIVE KIDS, ages 8-17, wave and shout goodbye.

GEORGE	GEORGE'S KIDS
So long . . .! Patty, I'll see you Wednesday? So long, Lee!	Goodbye, Patrick! See ya, Patrick! Bye, Patty! G'bye!

JANINE	PATRICK
So long . . .!	'Bye guys! Yeah, Wednesday! G'bye!

INT. LEE'S CAR (MOVING). NIGHT.

LEE and PATRICK get in the car and start driving.

> LEE
>
> How's the motor?

> PATRICK
>
> George says the piston's gonna go right through the block any minute now.

> LEE
>
> Unfortunately that's a problem. We can't afford to keep the boat if we can't hire somebody to work it, and we can't get anyone to work it, if it's got a broken motor.

> PATRICK
>
> Let's take out a loan.

> LEE
>
> And pay it back with what?

> PATRICK
>
> We hire it out 'til we pay the loan back, obviously.

> LEE
>
> Unfortunately for you, I'm responsible for your finances until you're twenty-one, and I'm not comfortable takin' out enormous loans on your behalf right now.

PATRICK

I have band practice. Can you drive
me home to get my stuff and then
drive me to Sandy's house?

LEE

Why don't you sign up for driver's ed?

PATRICK   LEE *(Cont'd.)*
Because Dad made me   I'm not your chauffeur.
promise not to drive 'til I
was seventeen.

LEE *(Cont'd.)*
OK. Then we'll stick with that.

EXT. SANDY & JILL'S HOUSE. NIGHT.
LEE's car idles in front of the house.

PATRICK

You wanna stay for dinner? I think
Sandy's mother likes you.

LEE

No she doesn't.

PATRICK

Yes she does. This could be good for
both of us.

LEE

I'd really rather not.

PATRICK

Well, can you at least hang out with
her so I can be alone with Sandy for
half an hour without her mother
knockin' on the door every twenty
seconds?

LEE   PATRICK *(Cont'd.)*
Come on, man.   All you gotta do is talk to
                                 her! Why can't you help me
                                 out a little bit for once

                                   PATRICK *(Cont'd.)*
                          instead of draggin' me to
                          the lawyers and the funeral
                          parlor and the morgue?
                          Anyway she's really nice!

                              LEE
          OK.

                              PATRICK
          Thank you.

INT. SANDY'S HOUSE—BASEMENT. NIGHT.

PATRICK is practicing with his band. SANDY on lead vocals, the guys singing backup.

                              SANDY
                    "Tell me why—Why do you need me?
                    Why do you want me? / Why do you
                    love me?"

                              PATRICK
          Stop. Stop.

Everybody stops playing.

                          PATRICK *(Cont'd.)*
          Otto, man—

                              OTTO
          What? I'm too slow?

                              CJ
          Too fast.

                              OTTO
          I'm too fast?

                              JOEL
          Dude, you're like pullin' outta the
          fuckin' station ahead of me.

                              SANDY
          Oh my God, you guys! Leave him
          alone.

                         CJ
Are you serious about this band or
what?

                        OTTO
Get off my back.

                         CJ
All right, everybody just chill here.
Let's just go again.

Everyone resets.

                      PATRICK
                (Into microphone.)
We are Stentorian.

INT. JILL'S LIVING ROOM. NIGHT.

LEE and JILL are alone in the living room. She has a glass of
wine. He has a beer. Silence.

                        JILL
Patrick's one of my favorite people.

                        LEE
That's good.

Silence. JILL twists around.

                        JILL
                (Calls up the stairs.)
How's it goin' up there, you guys?

Silence. Then there is some O.C. giggling and A DOOR OPENS.

SANDY   PATRICK
It's going fine! Thanks! But   Good! Really good! We're
we're right in the middle of   totally rippin' through those
something!   compound fractions!

There is more laughing and the DOOR SHUTS O.C.

                        JILL
At least we know where they are,
right?

LEE

That's true . . .

INT. SANDY'S ROOM. SIMULTANEOUS.

SANDY comes away from the door. They are in their underwear. PATRICK discards an unused, unrolled condom and GETS UP to get another from his pants, across the darkened room.

PATRICK

Hold on a sec.

SANDY

How many of those you generally gotta go through before you pick a winner?

PATRICK

I'd like to see you use one of these goddamn things with all these interruptions—Ow!

He trips over something with a crash.

SANDY

What happened? Are you OK?

PATRICK

I tripped over your fuckin' doll house.

SANDY

Oh my God, did you break it?

PATRICK

I don't know. *I'm* fine though, by the way.

SANDY snaps the light on.

SANDY

Oh my God. My grandmother gave me that when I was five years old. It was literally her doll house from when she was a little girl.

PATRICK

Well what's it doin' on the fuckin'
floor?

SANDY

It's a *doll* house! That's where you
play with it!

JILL *(O.S.)*

Sandy? What is going on up there?

SANDY

Nothing! Patrick stubbed his toe on
Mummer's doll house, but it's OK!

JILL

Sandy, that doll house belonged to
my *mother*!

SANDY	JILL *(Cont'd.)*
Yes I *know*, Mom! It was just an *accident*. Nobody's smashin' it to pieces! It's fine!	If you're gonna smash it to pieces I wish you'd let me keep it somewhere else!

PATRICK

Don't worry, Jill, I'm OK!
My toe's gonna be OK!

INT. LIVING ROOM. NIGHT—CONTINUOUS.

JILL turns back to LEE, smiles and shrugs. Silence.

JILL

Could I get you another beer, Lee?

LEE

I'm good. Thanks.

JILL sips her wine. LEE can't think of anything to say.

JILL

Would you excuse me, Lee, one sec?

LEE

Sure.

INT. SANDY'S ROOM. CONTINUOUS.

The only light comes from SANDY's laptop. They're on the bed.

                    SANDY
          Is it on?

                    PATRICK
          Yes. It's a miracle.

                    SANDY
          OK. Hurry up.

JILL KNOCKS. PATRICK and SANDY leap away from each other.

            JILL   SANDY *(Cont'd.)*
Hey, Sandy? I'm sorry . . .!   One second please! *(To*
                                    PATRICK.*)* Get outta my way!
            PATRICK
Goddamn it!

AT THE DOOR, A MOMENT LATER—JILL is talking to SANDY
through a crack in the door. PATRICK is pretending to work at
the laptop. SANDY and he have pulled on their clothes.

                    SANDY
          What's up?

                    JILL
          I'm really sorry, I know you're trying
          to work, but I can't sit down there
          much longer.

                    SANDY
          Why? What's the problem?

                    JILL
          He won't *talk*. I've been trying to
          make conversation for half an hour!

                    SANDY
          Are you serious?

            JILL   PATRICK
I realize I'm not the most   What's the matter?
fascinating person in the
world, but it's very, very   SANDY
strained.   Mom . . .

SANDY

She can't make your Uncle speak.

PATRICK

He likes sports.

JILL	SANDY
I'm sorry to bust things up, but how much longer do you think you're gonna be? I'm sorry . . . !	Sports?

PATRICK

Can you talk about sports? Maybe there's a game on you could watch.

SANDY *(To* PATRICK.*) (Cont'd.)*

Shut up. *(To* JILL.*)* Mummy, Please.

INT. LEE'S CAR (MOVING) NIGHT.

LEE drives PATRICK home.

PATRICK

You were a tremendous help.

LEE

I didn't ask to sit down there.

PATRICK

You can't make small talk like every other grown up in the world?

PATRICK *(Cont'd.)*	LEE
You can't talk about boring bullshit for half an hour? "Hey, how about those interest rates?" Hey, I lost my Triple A card?" Like everybody else?	No. Nope. Sorry.

PATRICK

You're a fuckin' asshole.

INT. PATRICK'S ROOM. NIGHT.

PATRICK is having trouble sleeping.

EXT/INT. LEE'S CAR (MOVING). DAY.

LEE is driving PATRICK along the road to Essex.

> LEE
>
> Where did she say she lives? Because there are like no houses here. None. Does she live in a fuckin' sleeping bag?

> PATRICK
>
> 119 Pigeon Hill Street.

> LEE
>
> Pigeon Hill Street? Or Pigeon Hill Road? Pigeon Hill Court?

> PATRICK *(Cont'd.)*
>
> Pigeon Hill Street. Street! This is Pigeon Hill Road.

> PATRICK *(Cont'd.)*
>
> You have no GPS whatsoever?

> LEE
>
> No, I've got a little fuckin' cartoon moving map.

> PATRICK
>
> Do you want me to punch it in for you?

> LEE
>
> No, I don't. I've got it. Thank you. *(Pause.)* Okay, listen. Are you nervous?

> PATRICK
>
> Yeah I'm nervous.

> PATRICK *(Cont'd.)*
>
> What are you, a fuckin' genius?

> LEE
>
> Because—
> Skip it.

> LEE *(Cont'd.)*
>
> Just . . . If anything gets weird, just text me, and I'll come and get you.

> PATRICK
>
> OK. *(Pause.)* Thank you.

EXT. ELISE'S HOUSE. DAY.

They pull up to a small neatly kept house and get out. ELISE opens the front door. She looks starched and brittle.

> ELISE
>
> Oh my gosh. Is that my Patrick?

> PATRICK
>
> Hi Mom.

> ELISE
>
> I'm so happy . . .! *(To* LEE.*)* Welcome to my home.

INT. ELISE'S HOUSE. CONTINUOUS.

JEFFREY stands waiting as ELISE ushers them in. He is in his late 40s, slight, well groomed and dressed in conservative weekend wear. Slacks, loafers, a light-weight sweater. LEE glances around the very tidy house. There is a framed pastel of Jesus on the wall.

> ELISE
>
> Patrick. This is my fella. Jeffrey, this is Patrick . . .

> JEFFREY
>
> *(Shaking hands.)*
>
> Great to finally meet you, Patrick.

> PATRICK
>
> Nice to meet you.

> ELISE
>
> And this is Lee . . .

> JEFFREY
>
> *(Shaking hands.)*
>
> Hey, welcome. Jeffrey.

> LEE
>
> Thanks. Lee.

> ELISE
>
> Now, Lee, are you sure you won't stay for lunch?

                    LEE
I'm positive.

INT. ELISE'S DINING NOOK. DAY.

PATRICK is at the table. JEFFREY and ELISE bring in lunch.

                    PATRICK
Oh—Can I help with anything?

                    ELISE
No thanks, honey.

                    JEFFREY
Your job is to relax. OK? That is your
A-Number One assignment.

                    PATRICK
OK. I'm gonna really apply myself.

                    JEFFREY
No—I was just joking.

                    PATRICK
I know you were. So was I.

ELISE comes in from the kitchen and sits down.

                    ELISE
How we gettin' along?

                    JEFFREY
Great.

                    PATRICK
Great.

                    ELISE
You don't have to be so polite, you
know!

                    PATRICK
Oh—I'm not bein' polite . . .

                    ELISE
Did you wanna wash your hands
before we eat?

PATRICK

Um—Yeah.

INT. ELISE'S DINING ROOM. DAY.

Everyone is seated. JEFFREY is saying grace.

JEFFREY

For what we are about to receive let
us give thanks. Amen.

ELISE   PATRICK

Amen.   Amen.

They start passing around the lunch.

ELISE

It's OK to say Amen, Patrick . . .!
Nobody's tryin' to *recruit* you!

PATRICK

I did say Amen.

ELISE

You did? OK. You don't have to . . .

PATRICK

I know. I just said it really quietly.

ELISE

Honey, it's fine. I know—I'm gonna
be a shock to you. In a lotta ways.
Hopin' it's a *good* shock . . .

PATRICK

Yeah . . .

JEFFREY

What can I get you, Patrick?

ELISE

I hope everything's OK . . .
    (e.g. the lunch.)

PATRICK

Oh yeah, it looks great. Thank you.

ELISE

You don't have to be so formal . . .!

PATRICK

I'm not.

JEFFREY	ELISE
I think Elise's just—	I know . . .! I'm just sayin', this is your home too! I want it to be . . . It's different from what you're *used* to, but . . .
PATRICK	And . . . I don't know . . .!
That's OK . . .	

JEFFREY

What are you studying in school, Patrick?

PATRICK

Oh . . . well . . . The usual stuff . . .

ELISE

You know what? I'm gonna be right back. Anybody need anything from the kitchen?

JEFFREY	PATRICK
I think we're good. No.	No, thanks. Thank you.

ELISE gets up and goes into the kitchen.

JEFFREY

Did you get some string beans?

PATRICK

Oh—not yet. Thank you.

JEFFREY

OK. *(Pause.)* Lemme just see what she's doin' in there.

He goes into the kitchen. PATRICK eats.

INT. LEE'S CAR (MOVING) DUSK.

LEE is driving PATRICK home. He glances at PATRICK. PATRICK is very glum and unhappy.

> LEE
>
> So what was she like?

> PATRICK
>
> I don't know: She was pretty
> nervous.

> LEE
>
> What was the guy like?

> PATRICK
>
> He was very Christian.

LEE	PATRICK *(Cont'd.)*
You know we're Christian too, right? You are aware that Catholics are Christians?	Yes, I know that. Yes I am aware of that.

They drive in gloomy silence.

> LEE
>
> Well . . . it sounds like she's doin'
> better anyway. She's not drinkin'.
> She's not in the psych ward.

> PATRICK
>
> Wow.

LEE	PATRICK *(Cont'd.)*
Wow *what*?	You'll do *anything* to get ridda me!

> LEE
>
> What?

> PATRICK
>
> You heard me.

> LEE
>
> That's not true.

PATRICK shrugs and starts texting on his iPhone.

INT. PATRICK'S ROOM. NIGHT.

PATRICK sits at his laptop, wet from the shower. He opens an email from *JEFFGARNDER7@YAHOO.COM*. We see the first few lines and hear JEFFREY's VOICE at the same time.

> JEFFREY *(V.O.)*
> *"Dear Patrick, I'm writing on to thank*
> *you for today. Your visit meant the*
> *world to your mom. We are both deeply*
> *grateful for the love and trust you've*
> *shown by offering to rejoin her life.*
> *But I feel it would be unfair to your*
> *mom to rush her along the long and*
> *challenging road ahead, and so I'm*
> *going to ask you to write to me in*
> *future to arrange any further visits.*
> *I hope you won't find this to be—"*

ON PATRICK as he reads on. He DELETES THE MESSAGE.

INT. LIVING ROOM. NIGHT.

PATRICK is watching an action movie on TV. LEE drifts in.

> LEE
> Where's your friends tonight?

> PATRICK
> I don't know.

> LEE
> Why don't you call that girl Sandy and
> see if she'll come over?

> PATRICK
> No thanks. Nice try, though.

(Pause.) LEE walks away and goes into—

INT. JOE'S DEN. NIGHT.

LEE turns on the light. He walks over to the fancy GUN CASE.
It's got several expensive rifles mounted, and some HANDGUNS.
LEE gets the key from on top of the case and opens it. He
takes out a HANDGUN. Realizes that PATRICK is in the doorway.

> PATRICK
> Who are you gonna shoot? You or me?

                    LEE
Do you know how much these guns
are worth?

                    PATRICK
A lot, I think.

                    LEE
Want to try to sell them and put the
money toward a new second hand
motor for the boat?

                    PATRICK
That's a really good idea.

EXT. GUN SHOP. DAY.

Through the window we see LEE and PATRICK talking to the
GUN SHOP OWNER. JOE's guns are laid out on the counter on
a felt cloth. The OWNER is counting out bills for them.

EXT. MARINA—BOAT YARD. DAY.

LEE, GEORGE and PATRICK are connecting up the new second-
hand MOTOR to JOE's BOAT.

                    PATRICK
    This is awesome.

EXT. JOE'S BOAT (MOVING)—AT SEA. DAY.

A beautiful day at sea. PATRICK is driving the boat, fast.
SANDY is next to him. LEE is in the back, taking in the air.

                    SANDY
    This is awesome!

                    PATRICK
You wanna drive?

                    SANDY
Sure!

                    PATRICK
OK—So—

The BOAT SWERVES WILDLY as SANDY takes the wheel.

PATRICK (*Cont'd.*)	SANDY
Yeah—Don't—Just	(*Screams.*)
straighten her out—OK.	Oh my God! Sorry!

She straightens the wheel and speeds up again.

EXT. JOE'S DRIVEWAY. DAY.

LEE drives SANDY and PATRICK into the driveway and stops.
SANDY and PATRICK get out of the car.

> LEE
> I gotta run some chores. I'll be back in
> a couple hours. You want anything?

PATRICK	SANDY
No thank you.	No thanks Mr. Chandler.

LEE drives away.

> SANDY (*Cont'd.*)
> Setup city.

> PATRICK
> What are you talking about?

> SANDY
> Oh yeah? How's Silvie McGann?

> PATRICK
> Who?!

> SANDY
> Open the door.

INT. PATRICK'S BEDROOM. DAY.

SANDY and PATRICK lie on the bed, her dozing head on his
chest. He's very happy.

EXT. WATERFRONT STREET. DAY.

LEE is walking toward his car. He slows because he sees
RANDI pushing a stroller his way, with a newborn BABY in it.
The baby is almost invisible inside his winter parka. RANDI
is accompanied by a friend, RACHEL, 40s.

                    RANDI

Lee . . .! Hi.

                    LEE

Hi.

                    RANDI

Um—Rachel. This is Lee. Lee,
Rachel.

                    LEE

Hi.

                    RACHEL

Hello.

                    RANDI
              (Re: the baby.)
And this is Dylan. You can't see him
too good.

                    LEE

Hey Dylan. Very handsome.

                    RACHEL

Randi, you want me to get the car
and pick you up?

        RANDI   LEE
Oh, sure—   That's OK. I gotta—

                    RANDI

Well, could I—I'd—Could we talk a
second?

                    LEE

Sure.

                    RACHEL

I'll just pull around—Just be like two
minutes.

                    RANDI

OK, thanks.

                    RACHEL

Nice to meet you.

LEE
You too.

RACHEL
Be right back.

RACHEL hurries off and turns a corner.

RANDI
I don't have anything big to say:

RANDI (*Cont'd.*)	LEE
I just—I know you been around—	That's OK.
	Yeah, I just been gettin'
And I thought—we never—	Patrick settled in.
Yeah I know. He seems like	
he's doin' pretty well,	
considering. I mean . . .	I *think* he is . . . Yeah . .

RANDI
I guess you probably didn't know I
really kept in touch with Joe—

RANDI (*Cont'd.*)	LEE
So it's been kinda weird for	No, I knew that—
me, not seeing Patrick since	
he passed away—Oh, OK. I	
didn't know.	

LEE (*Cont'd.*)
Well you can see him. I have no—

RANDI
Could we ever have lunch?

LEE
You mean us? You and me?

RANDI
Yeah. I, uh . . . Because . . . I said a
lotta terrible things to you. But—I
know you never—Maybe you don't
wanna talk to me—

LEE

It's not that.

RANDI

But let me finish. However it—my heart was broken. It's always gonna be broken. I know your heart is broken too. But I don't have to carry . . . I said things that I should—I should fuckin' burn in hell for what I said. It was just—

LEE

No, no . . .

RANDI

I'm just sorry. I love you. Maybe I shouldn't say that. And I'm sorry—

LEE *(Cont'd.)*

I can't—

You can say it, but—No, it's just—I—I can't—I gotta go.

RANDI

We couldn't have lunch?

LEE

I'm really sorry. I don't think so.

RANDI

You can't just *die* . . .!

But honey, I see you walkin' around like this and I just wanna tell you—

But Lee, you gotta—I don't know what! I don't wanna torture you. I just wanna tell you I was wrong.

That's not true! Can't be true . . .!

LEE *(Cont'd.)*

Thank you for sayin' everything—I'm not! But I can't—I'm happy for you. And I want . . . I would want to talk to you—But I can't, I can't . . .

I'm tryin' to—You're not. But I got nothin' to— Thank you for sayin' that. But—There's nothin' there . . . You don't understand . . .

                    RANDI
          Of course I do!

                     LEE
          I know you understand . . . But I've
          gotta go—I'm sorry.

          RANDI   LEE (*Cont'd.*)
OK. I'm sorry.   There's nothin' I can s—
                        I gotta go.

He moves away. RANDI breaks down.

INT. WATERFRONT BAR & GRILLE. DAY.

CU LEE, very drunk. He is at the counter of a busy local place
full of FISHERMEN eating and drinking their lunch. A new
bunch of guys comes in loudly and boisterously. One of them
accidentally clips LEE as the group passes by.

                  FISHERMAN
          Pardon me.

                     LEE
          It's all right.
LEE whirls around and sucker punches the FISHERMAN. He
goes down hard. His friends immediately grab at LEE en masse.

                  FISHERMEN
          Hey! Hey! What're you doin'? Etc.

LEE is pushed into some tables—The whole place is in an
uproar—He is jumped by several guys. He keeps fighting
crazily. Someone tries to pin his arms to stop the fight.
Everyone is shouting.

GEORGE appears. He uses his size to shove the other guys
away from LEE.

                   GEORGE
          Break it up! Break it up! It's Lee
          Chandler. Lee! Let him go, Eddy.
          He's Joey Chandler's brother. Let
          him go! Lee. Lee! It's George. Lee.

Come on—*(To the guys who beat* LEE
up.) You won. OK? You won the fight.

LEE shoves GEORGE away and swings at the nearest man.
Everybody pounces on him again. Someone hits LEE squarely
and knocks him down. Now GEORGE is fighting everybody.
Chaos.

> GEORGE *(Cont'd.)*
> OK, OK, OK!

INT. GEORGE'S LIVING ROOM. DAY.

LEE is dazed, lying on the sofa in GEORGE's cramped living
room. GEORGE watches anxiously as GEORGE's wife JANINE
finishes washing and bandaging LEE's banged up face.
GEORGE is a little banged up too.

> JANINE
> . . . Should we take him to the
> hospital?

> GEORGE
> I don't think so. Nothin's broken.

> JANINE
> . . . What the hell did they hit him
> with, a fuckin' baseball bat?

> GEORGE
> They all just said he started swingin'.

LEE wakes up.

> LEE
> Where's Patrick?

> GEORGE
> He's with the kids. I sent 'em out for
> burgers.

> LEE
> Lemme give you some money.

LEE sits up painfully and reaches for his wallet.

> GEORGE
> Lee. Please. It's my treat.

LEE stands up and fumbles for his wallet and drops it on the floor. GEORGE picks it up and gives it to him.

> GEORGE *(Cont'd.)*
> Would you sit down please, for
> Christ's sake?

> LEE
> OK.

LEE sits down and breaks into tears.

> GEORGE
> Come on, buddy.

GEORGE looks uncomfortable. He looks up toward the kitchen. JANINE comes back in with coffee and sits next to LEE.

> LEE
> I'm sorry . . .

> GEORGE
> That's OK, buddy. It's OK . . .

> JANINE
> Lee? Have some coffee. Come on.
> Drink this . . .

LEE takes the coffee and keeps crying. GEORGE and JANINE exchange a look.

INT. JOE'S HOUSE—KITCHEN. NIGHT.

PATRICK comes in, followed by LEE. LEE moves slowly past him into the living room.

INT. JOE'S ROOM. NIGHT.

PATRICK walks in and takes a long look at LEE's THREE FRAMED PHOTOS.

INT. LIVING ROOM. NIGHT.

LEE lies on the sofa nursing a beer, his face swollen and cut. PATRICK comes in from the kitchen and hovers.

> PATRICK
>
> Can I get you anything, Uncle Lee?

> LEE
>
> No thanks, buddy.

> PATRICK
>
> OK. I'm goin' to bed.

> LEE
>
> Good night.

EXT. JOE'S HOUSE—DAY.

The sun shines over the house, the town, and the water.

INT. JOE'S HOUSE—KITCHEN. DAY.

LEE puts some spaghetti sauce in a skillet and turns the flame on.

INT. LIVING ROOM. DAY.

LEE is asleep on the sofa with a beer while the TV plays . . . A LITTLE HAND tugs at his SLEEVE.

> SUZY *(O.C.)*
>
> Daddy?

He turns his head and sees without surprise his DAUGHTERS seated next to him in their nightgowns. The BABY is in a playpen on the floor. SUZY, 7, is pulling his sleeve. LEE smiles at them.

> LEE
>
> Yes, honey?

> SUZY
>
> Can't you see we're burning?

> LEE
>
> No, honey . . . You're not burning.

LEE WAKES UP—There's SMOKE coming from the KITCHEN.

INT. KITCHEN. DAY.

The blackened skillet is SMOKING. LEE comes in and puts it under the water in the sink. It hisses and steams.

> PATRICK *(O.S.)*
> Uncle Lee! What the hell's that
> smell?

> LEE
> I just burnt the sauce! Everything's
> OK!

He grips the sink and tries to recover from his dream.

INT. LEE'S CAR (MOVING) NIGHT.

LEE drives up GEORGE and JANINE's street.

INT. GEORGE'S HOUSE. DAY.

PUSH IN: (MOS) LEE is seated at the dining table talking seriously with GEORGE and JANINE. It has the air of a conference.

INT. LIVING ROOM. NIGHT.

LEE and PATRICK eat dinner.

> LEE
> I got a job in Boston. It starts in July.

> PATRICK
> What is it?

> LEE
> Custodian, handyman . . . But just
> two buildings this time.

> PATRICK
> And what delightful Boston neighborhood have you selected for us to
> live in?

> LEE
> None.

> PATRICK
> What do you mean?

> LEE
> You don't have to move to Boston.
> I'm gonna be in Charlestown and
> George is gonna take you.

PATRICK

What?

LEE

Yeah. I talked to them last week.
I explained the situation to them.
Georgie Junior's goin' to school this
fall. Jimmy graduates next year. We'll
have to rent out this house. You can
move back in when you turn eighteen.
When you turn twenty-one, you're allowed to sell it or stay in it, or whatever
you want. Definitely have to hire the
boat out when the summer's over—just
like we talked about. I thought when
you get your license, we can figure that
one out as we go. I'm still the trustee,
but all the financial stuff Joe set up for
me is gonna get transferred over to
George. So everything'll be the same,
except you don't have to move.

PATRICK

But . . . like, are they gonna be my
guardians? Or do you still—

LEE

They're gonna adopt you. *(Pause.)*
Anyway, that's how I set it up. If you
want. It's up to you.

PATRICK	LEE *(Cont'd.)*
So are you gonna just disappear?	You don't have to do it. No. No. I just set it up so you can stay here. They're really glad to have you. They love you.

PATRICK

I know. I mean, they're great . . . But
why can't you stay?

PATTY starts crying.

> LEE
>
> Come on, Patty . . . I can't beat it.
> *(Pause.)* I can't beat it. I'm sorry.

PATRICK wipes his eyes. LEE comes over and hugs him.

EXT. MANCHESTER STREET/ROSEDALE CEMETERY. DAY.

PATRICK walks along the street. The TREES he passes have BUDS or BLOSSOMS. It's early SPRING. He snaps a dead branch off a tree. He runs it across a fence as he walks. We REVEAL that he is headed for the cemetery gate. He goes into the cemetery.

He pokes his stick into the ground to see if it's softened up. It has. He digs up some clods. He walks away.

EXT. AN OLD MANCHESTER HOUSE. DAY.

A MILNE PLUMBING & HEATING VAN is parked in the driveway.

INT. BASEMENT. DAY.

LEE is kneeling on the floor in coveralls, working on the hotwater heater. The HOMEOWNER, in his 80s, stands by watching.

> HOMEOWNER
>
> What do you think?

> LEE
>
> I think you're gonna be OK.

> HOMEOWNER
>
> Are you one of Stan Chandler's boys?

> LEE
>
> Yeah, I'm Lee.

> HOMEOWNER
>
> I used to play a little chess with your father a long time ago. He was a heck of a chess player.

> LEE
>
> That's him.

> HOMEOWNER
> He's not still living, is he?

> LEE
> No.

> HOMEOWNER
> And one of the sons passed away
> recently I heard.

> LEE
> Yeah. Joe. My brother.

> HOMEOWNER
> That's right. Very personable man.

> LEE
> Yeah.

> HOMEOWNER
> My father passed away in 1959. A
> young man. Worked on a tuna boat.
> Went out one morning, little bit of
> weather, nothing dramatic . . . And he
> never returned. No signal. No Mayday.
> No one ever knew what happened.

LEE continues to work on the heater.

EXT. LAWYER'S OFFICE WINDOW. DAY.

Past the BLOSSOMS on the tree outside Wes's window, we see
GEORGE, LEE and WES, signing documents.

EXT. JOE'S HOUSE. DAY.

There is a "FOR RENT BY OWNER" SIGN outside the house.
LEE's car is in the yard. Also PATRICK's bicycle.

EXT. CEMETERY. DAY.

(MOS) Joe's burial service. PATRICK, LEE, GEORGE and JANINE
all stand in a row at the front. RANDI holds a CRYING BABY.
She gives him to JOSH, who steps away.

CU: CHANDLER TOMBSTONE. Engraved are the names of
LEE's parents and now JOE.

EXT. WIDE SHOT OF THE TOWN. DAY.

A beautiful early spring day. Lots of boats in the water.

EXT. MANCHESTER STREET—CORNER GROCERY STORE. DAY.

LEE and PATRICK walk up the street, still in their funeral clothes.

> PATRICK
> I'm gonna get some ice cream.

> LEE
> Go ahead.

> PATRICK
> Can I have some money?

> LEE
> Yeah.

LEE gives him a ten-dollar bill. PATRICK goes inside. LEE picks up an old rubber ball from the ground and bounces it up and down. PATRICK comes out with an ice cream bar.

EXT. MANCHESTER STREET. DAY.

LEE and PATRICK trudge up a steeply inclined street. LEE occasionally bounces the ball.

> PATRICK
> So . . . When am I supposed to move in with Georgie?

> LEE
> July. I don't even have a place to live yet.

> PATRICK
> Don't they give you an apartment?

> LEE
> Yeah, but I was gonna try to get a

place with an extra room. Or room
for like a pullout sofa.

> PATRICK

What for?

> LEE

In case you wanna visit sometime. Or
if you're lookin' at colleges in Boston
or somethin' and you wanna stay
overnight . . .

> PATRICK

I'm not goin' to college.

> LEE

All right, well then I'll have an extra
room for all my *shit*. Do we have to
talk about this now?

> PATRICK

Nope.

He tosses away his ice cream stick.

After a minute LEE wipes his eyes. He bounces the ball and
tosses it to PATRICK. It goes wide and bounces crazily.

> PATRICK *(Cont'd.)*

Great throw.

> LEE

Just let it go.

PATRICK runs to gets the ball. They continue to walk up the
hill, bouncing the ball across the street to each other and
chasing it when it rolls back down the hill.

EXT. WIDE SHOT OF THE TOWN—JOE'S BOAT. DAY.

LEE and PATRICK head out to fish. PATRICK drives the boat.

LEE sets up the fishing gear.

A FEW MOMENTS LATER—LEE and PATRICK are seated, fishing off the back of the boat. They talk quietly. LEE looks a little better than we've seen him. He squints at the sea and the wide open sky.

FADE OUT.

THE END